# The Sheikh's Convenient Virgin

## TRISH MOREY

**Trish Morey** is an Australian who's also spent time living and working in New Zealand and England. Now she's settled with her husband and four young daughters in a special part of South Australia, surrounded by orchards and bushland, and visited by the occasional koala and kangaroo. With a life-long love of reading, she penned her first book at age eleven, after which life, career and a growing family kept her busy until once again she could indulge her desire to create characters and stories—this time in romance. Having her work published is a dream come true. Visit Trish at her website, www.trishmorey.com

To Jacqui, Steph, Ellen and Claire

Thanks for all the times you've had to wait for me to finish a sentence, a paragraph or a chapter before you could get my attention.

And thanks for all the times you had to do lots of extra stuff because I was on deadline and the house would have collapsed in a heap otherwise.

Not to mention all the times you forgave me for forgetting to pick you up from wherever. (Really sorry about those!)

But, most of all, thank you all for being your totally gorgeous selves.

I am truly blessed.

All my love,

Mum
xxxx

# CHAPTER ONE

'WHO'S the woman?' With just three sharp words Sheikh Tajik al Zayed bin Aman cut off the tedious update being delivered by his secretary as he wandered closer to the window. It had been a long flight, and the stranger he'd just spied sitting near the pool was far more interesting than the latest exchange rate fluctuations of his Emirate's currency. 'What is she doing here?'

Kamil temporarily abandoned his recitation of numbers and followed his ruler's gaze through the wall of windows and past the palm-lined lawns to the pool area beyond.

'This is the one we employed as your mother's companion after Fatima was taken ill. I sent word to you while you were in Paris for the oil summit…' His secretary trailed off, suddenly hesitant, as if concerned he'd overstepped the mark in retaining a local woman to be Nobilah's companion during their Gold Coast sojourn.

'Ah, yes,' Tajik said, recalling the case of appendicitis that had seen Fatima packed off to hospital for emergency surgery. 'I just did not expect Nobilah's new companion to be quite so young.' *Or quite so attractive.* Even from this distance he could see her features were far from plain, her figure, even though demurely dressed from neck to ankle in light trousers and shirt, no chore to behold. 'So why is she alone and not looking after my mother?'

As if on cue, Nobilah emerged from the poolhouse behind, the dark abaya she'd favoured since her husband had died swirling about her like a cloud as she walked. He watched the younger woman rise and then adjust the umbrella shading his mother from the Queensland sun as she settled herself into the chair alongside. Then the young woman sat back down, picking up a newspaper from a wrought-iron table sitting between them, her lips moving as she read aloud.

His mother laughed at something, and he could almost hear her musical chuckle. He couldn't help but smile. It had been a tough year—for all of them—and it was good to see her laugh. Very soon he would hear it for himself. After the tense and at times heated negotiations of the past week he deserved it. And now they would have the last weeks of their summer break together.

'I must go and let Nobilah know I have returned from Paris,' he said over his shoulder. 'Was there anything more, Kamil?'

His secretary cleared his throat. 'As a matter of fact, Excellency, there is one more item I must bring to your attention…'

'Can it wait? I am anxious to catch up with my mother.'

'I think you will want to hear this, Excellency.'

Tajik looked around in surprise. His secretary knew him too well to keep him over some trifling matter when he was already taking his leave. He moved away from the window, his attention now fully on his secretary, the stranger all but dismissed from his mind. 'Well, what is it?'

'There have been murmurings from home… It appears

Qasim has raised with the council of tribal leaders some concerns about the ascendancy...'

Tajik's blood chilled at the news, but it was to Kamil that his ire was directed right now. 'And you thought it more important to relate Jamalbad's exchange rates than my cousin's machinations behind the scenes?'

His secretary had the good sense to look nervous. 'Reports have just come in,' he said, bowing deferentially. 'They have yet to been confirmed—'

'Then have them confirmed!' he snapped as he began pacing the spacious living area in long purposeful strides. 'And tell me why should my cousin bring such concerns to the council? If anything happens to me, he knows he is next in line to the throne. His place is assured.'

'He has apparently told the council members he believes Jamalbad's future cannot be assured unless there is solid provision for the future. Unless there is an heir.'

Tajik's feet came to a sudden halt. 'My father has been dead but one short year, and Joharah with him! Would Qasim have me casting my seed at the first woman to cross my path? Besides, everyone knows that my cousin is more an agent of instability than of peace—otherwise why would he be stirring up trouble while my back is turned?'

'Qasim cloaks his desire for the throne in concerns for Jamalbad. Some of the council will take his words at face value.'

'And some members of the council would be swayed by the dance of the cobra.' Tajik thumped his closed fist against the nearest piece of furniture with so much force it made his secretary jump. 'He must be stopped! If these reports are true, we must return to Jamalbad immediately. Prepare to make the necessary arrangements.'

Kamil hesitated. 'Before I do—there's one more thing you should know. There is a suggestion that he has told the council he has found you the perfect bride.'

'He has *what*? Who is the delightful creature this snake of a cousin of mine would see me saddled with?'

'His daughter, Abir.'

Tajik laughed out loud. 'In the name of Allah, the girl is but a child! She must be no more than ten years old. He wants the throne so badly he would sacrifice his own child to his cause?'

'Abir is fourteen at her next birthday. More than old enough to become betrothed if the council so approves.'

'Not to me, she's not! I will not be manipulated by a madman into marrying a child less than half my age, especially not his own spawn, merely to give him greater access to the throne.'

Kamil frowned. 'Beware, Excellency. From what's been said, some of the council are in favour of the match. They believe you have mourned long enough, that it is time you give away your playboy ways and find a bride to provide Jamalbad with an heir. Qasim has intimated that he is acting in your best interests, and that the best way forward for both you and Jamalbad is a betrothal announcement that is just days away.'

'So now a single life is to be interpreted as "playboy ways"?' He sighed. Given his age and his position he'd had his pick of women if and when he'd wanted—but losing Joharah had taken the edge off his needs, and the nameless and faceless women since then had been few and far between, his wants nowhere near approximating what those words implied.

He stared blindly out of the window, the blood hammering with fury in his veins. So Qasim meant to tie him into a betrothal in his absence—a betrothal he would be neatly boxed into on his return? No wonder his belligerent cousin had been so accommodating when Tajik had informed him of his plans to take his mother away from Jamalbad's month of horror heat to the relative cool of tropical Australia.

But there was no way he would allow himself to be manipulated like that. And there was no way he would marry his cousin's teenaged daughter. No way in the world.

He raked his fingers through his hair as he set about pacing the room once more, his mind working out the best strategy to outplay his cousin's hand. On the one hand he could just say no. He was absolute ruler of Jamalbad after all. The council was a powerful body in its own right, but it could only advise, not decree, and while it might not be happy with his refusal to marry Abir, it could not force him to do otherwise.

And yet there was another course of action that formed like crystals in his mind, clear and sharp. Another way he could stop Qasim's machinations in their tracks *and* keep the council happy into the deal.

'No, Kamil,' he asserted, swinging around. 'I will not marry Abir. Or anyone else my cousin lines up for me.'

'Very well, Excellency. Once I receive confirmation that our information is correct, I will prepare a message to the council to that effect.'

'No, there is no need. If the council are expecting a bride, then the council will be satisfied. They will have their sheikha.'

'And how do you intend to achieve that if you will not marry Abir?'

'Simple, Kamil. I will find my own bride.'

'Your Excellency, are you serious?'

The look he shot his secretary was enough to make his servant stammer in apology, but he cut off his backtracking with the simple act of raising one hand. 'I am serious about not being controlled like a puppet by my cousin. I will do whatever it takes to foil his plans to take over the throne of Jamalbad by marrying me to his daughter.'

'But a bride... You cannot marry just anyone. The bride of a ruler of Jamalbad must be pure of mind and body.' The secretary wildly threw out his arms in a gesture of hopelessness. 'How do you expect to find such a gem here?'

It took no more than a raised eyebrow for Kamil's coffee-coloured skin to flush darker. 'Have you not seen the women on the beach?' he blustered in defence. 'I am not sure that the council would approve of such a queen.'

Tajik nodded in understanding as his thoughts drew him in the direction of the windows again. Tradition was important in Jamalbad, and while he had been educated long enough in the west to believe that the idea a woman must remain untouched until marriage while the man was free to sow his wild oats wherever he chose was a classic double standard, the council would expect his bride to be innocent. Still, he was sure he could find someone who would pass for a *convenient virgin* somewhere. So long as he was happy with the choice, he would have no trouble convincing the council of her virtue.

He turned his gaze out of the windows once more, movement poolside bringing his gaze back into focus— and his thoughts into razor-sharp precision behind it.

She was quite attractive, in a western kind of way, her figure indeed watchable, despite the conservative clothes and the honey-blonde hair restrained too tightly behind her head. She would look so much better in more feminine clothes that showed off her curves. But then, given the truth of what Kamil had said, her conservatism was a definite plus right now...

He stroked his chin while he considered the possibilities. Fair-skinned, with honey-blonde hair and a generous mouth, she looked nothing at all like Joharah. That could only be a plus.

He clamped down on a twinge of guilt that he should be contemplating marrying *anyone*. But this would not be a marriage as theirs would have been. This marriage would be one of simple expediency that would put paid to Qasim's plans for the throne and bring stability to Jamalbad as a result.

Reason enough for him to contemplate the enjoyment he'd get presenting this woman as his bride. Her looks were merely a bonus. And bedding her would be no chore. He was a man, after all. He could certainly think of less enjoyable ways to foil his cousin's plans.

'Perhaps, Kamil,' he mused, 'we need not extend our search as far as the beach. Tell me,' he said, pointing to the young woman who had abandoned her reading of the newspaper and was currently engaged in painting his mother's nails, 'have you done all the necessary security checks on this woman?'

It wasn't really a question. He knew the answer would be in the affirmative—she wouldn't have been employed otherwise—and the older man looked confused at the sudden change of topic.

'Of course. She has a clean record, impeccable references, and no unsavoury connections that we could find.'

'And personally?'

'No attachments. As far as family she has just the one sister, a twin, recently married and with her first child.'

'Perfect,' Tajik announced coldly. 'Then she will not be missed.'

'What do you mean?' Kamil asked, with the tone of someone who really didn't want to hear the answer.

Tajik placed a hand on his secretary's shoulder. 'It's quite simple, my good friend. In finding my mother the perfect companion you have also done your country a great service. You may also have found Jamalbad the perfect queen.'

# CHAPTER TWO

'EXCELLENCY, this is madness. Taking a wife, taking a sheikha for your country, this is a serious matter.'

'You're right, Kamil,' he said with a brotherly slap on the back, 'and much too serious to be decided for me by the likes of my cousin.'

'But to decide on this woman on a whim, when the council cannot force you to marry Abir?'

'Listen, my good friend, do you think that if I refuse to marry Abir, Qasim will desist in his efforts to gain power? Of course he won't. He will keep working away, using whatever influence he has on the council for his own purposes.' He shrugged before continuing, 'And on one level Qasim and the council are right. Jamalbad needs an heir. And, sadly, I am in no position to provide them with an heir without a wife—a wife I simply have no interest in searching for.' He waved his hand in the direction of the window. 'Especially not when such an apparently suitable specimen sits just a few yards away. And she looks nothing like your "women on the beach". I am sure I can convince the council that she has all the necessary virtue she needs. Now, does this woman, this companion for my mother, have a name?'

His secretary was still shaking his head, but he could

no more refuse his ruler than stop breathing. 'Her name is Morgan Fielding, Excellency. But what makes you think, even if she were suitable for the role, that she would agree to marry you?'

Tajik laughed. The idea was preposterous. 'Come now, Kamil, she is a woman, and if you believe everything my cousin says I am a playboy through and through. With such a reputation, how could any woman resist me?'

Today was Gold Coast weather at its best: the sky an endless stretch of azure blue, bisected only by the occasional spear of jet stream, and with a slight breeze taking the edge off the sun's heat. Palm fronds swayed lazily in the gardens surrounding the pool, and diamonds of light played on the surface of the aqua water.

If a job could be perfect, then this one had to come close—relaxing days, beautiful surroundings, and nothing more taxing to do than keep a fascinating woman from an equally fascinating country company. She loved the stories Nobilah had told her about Jamalbad. She seemed to make the rich desert sunsets and the colours, scents and noise of the local soukhs come alive with her words.

Oh, yes, it was a dream job. Just a pity that it ended in less than two weeks. The gentle-faced Nobilah would return to Jamalbad and she would return to the temp agency. She sighed a wistful sigh. There was no way she could expect to be this lucky again. More likely she'd end up working ten hours a day for a madman in some office where the milk in the fridge lasted longer than the PAs.

Less than two weeks to go—so she'd just have to enjoy this experience while it lasted.

Morgan closed her eyes and breathed in deeply, the

scent of frangipani adding a heady sweetness to the air. If she tried hard she could almost imagine she was there, in Nobilah's home in Jamalbad, the desert-warmed air kissing her skin, the sweet scent of the palace orange grove tugging at her senses.

A shadow moved over her as the sun disappeared behind a cloud—until she remembered there were no clouds today, *and there should be no shadow*.

She snapped open her eyes with a start to see a man standing over her, a dark statue looming tall and powerful, his features indistinguishable with the wash of light behind. Without seeing his eyes she knew this man was a stranger. Without seeing his eyes she could still feel their impact like an acid burn. He was looking down at her. Staring. *Assessing*.

Her senses on trembling alert, she swung her legs over the edge of the chair, pushing herself to stand so as to remove at least some of the advantage he had by virtue of his height. But just standing was nowhere near enough. He still stood a full head above her, although at least from this angle she could finally see his eyes.

*And immediately regretted the fact.*

They burned gold, with scattered flecks like flaming coals, burning all the brighter with the contrast of his dark lashes and arched brows and the darkly shadowed angles of his cheeks and jaw.

Never before had she been confronted with someone so totally, unashamedly masculine. And never before had she felt more like an insect under a microscope. It was impossible not to resent his inspection. At the same time there was something compelling about those golden eyes that wouldn't let her turn away.

She swallowed, trying to quell the insane rush of sensation that coursed through her.

Attraction.

Desire.

*Fear.*

All those things rolled into one prickly surge of awareness as he silently continued to watch her.

'Can I help you?' she asked at last, when the silence had stretched out much longer than was polite, and it was clear he was not about to break it.

The corners of his mouth turned up, drawing her eyes to his full lips. And to a wide mouth she could tell immediately would be equally at home delivering either pleasure or pain. 'That is my intention,' he answered cryptically. But before she could think about a response, Nobilah stirred on the lounger alongside.

'Tajik! You're back already. Why didn't you tell me?'

He turned his attention to the much older woman, releasing the hold on Morgan's eyes as abruptly as the snapping of chains.

'The negotiations finished early,' he said, moving to the older woman's side and enclosing her in a bear-like hug that swept her off her feet and around in a circle of dark silk. 'I wanted to surprise you.'

'You did!' she said, her age-plumped features creasing in delight. 'I'm so pleased.'

Morgan watched the reunion, waiting for the perfect time to withdraw. So this was Nobilah's son, the Sheikh? She'd expected someone older, maybe forty or so, given that Nobilah was in her mid-sixties, but this man looked in his prime. He couldn't be more than early thirties. But then Nobilah had talked often of him as a child, of her dark haired boy who had grown up wild and untamed in the deserts of Jamalbad only to become a prince when her husband had unexpectedly came to the sheikhdom. Of the boy who had been torn from one life and thrown into another much more demanding and exacting.

As she looked at him now she could see no trace of that wild boy-child. Royalty was everything about him. His composure. His bearing. His sheer presence.

He could have been born to rule.

As if sensing her thoughts, he turned and captured her gaze. 'So this is your new companion?' he said, still holding his mother's hands in his own. 'So, tell me, is she any good?'

'Come and meet her,' his mother scolded, tugging him around. 'See for yourself.'

Morgan stiffened as he allowed his mother to lead him to the hired help. As if it was necessary. Surely he'd seen enough while he'd been standing over her? And if talking about her in the third person had been intended to make her feel uncomfortable, he'd sure hit the spot. She gave him a glare that should strip paint.

If he noticed her glare of disapproval he gave no hint of it. 'Morgan Fielding,' he uttered slowly—so slowly and deliberately, that the sound of her own name rolled through her, a strange, unfamiliar thing.

With an accent that was like a blend of the richest coffee and the darkest chocolate, he made her name sound good enough to eat. No, she corrected herself, catching sight of white teeth flashing between lips that looked too confident, too predatory, he made her name sound good enough to *devour*. She shivered. Because his eyes echoed the certainty. They looked down at her, their golden depths too knowing, too intent, as if he was reaching to some place deep inside her she hadn't known existed until now. And instinct warned her this man would do nothing by half measures.

And then he held out one hand, and she had no choice, no matter what her senses screamed to her in warning, but to do likewise.

She felt long fingers enclose her hand, circling around her wrist in a sensual dance of flesh against flesh as he drew her arm weightlessly towards him. With his eyes firmly fixed on hers she felt powerless to resist. Just when she thought he was intending to take her all the way to his lips, he stopped, and with the merest smile nodded slightly. 'It is indeed…a pleasure.'

Her heart thumping in her chest, it was all she could do to form, let alone hear, her own words. 'Sheikh Tajik, I've heard a lot about you.'

His smile widened, although his eyes remained steady, calculating.

'You have me at a distinct disadvantage,' he said. 'I know next to nothing of you—a failing I intend to rectify at the first opportunity, I assure you.'

Golden eyes told her he meant every word he said, while the gentle stroke of one long finger over her wrist sent tremors of heat reverberating up her arm.

'Taj,' Nobilah rebuked with a laugh, breaking the spell. 'Stop flirting with my companion. Come and tell me all about Paris. I'll send for tea.'

'I…I'll get it,' Morgan offered, smiling her thanks at Nobilah as she sensed a means of escape. She tugged her hand free and set off for the house, unable to ignore the prickle of heat on her skin, almost as if a pair of golden eyes were burning tracks into her back the whole way.

Nobilah had thought he'd been flirting with her? Why, then, had every word felt like some kind of threat? And why had the touch of his fingers on her flesh felt like some kind of promise?

She shivered again, wanting to shake off the unfamiliar sensations, and let herself into the house via the wide glass doors that led into the casual living areas and through to the kitchen beyond. She had almost crossed the cool tiled floor when she heard the voices—the even, low tones of Kamil and the raised voice of Anton, the chef they'd lured from one of Brisbane's top hotels for the duration of their stay.

'I have a contract,' the chef protested. 'I will not be sacked!'

Morgan pulled herself up short of the door. Obviously this was not a good time. But why were they sacking Anton? It made no sense. His cooking was three star Michelin standard, his menus superb. And Nobilah had made no secret of the fact that if she could she would like to take him back to Jamalbad with them.

'Not sacked,' she heard Kamil reply, his tone soothing yet insistent. 'The remaining balance owing on your contract will be paid in a lump sum, together with a generous bonus for any inconvenience.'

Anton grunted his displeasure and Morgan tuned out. She was turning to leave—right now was probably not the best time to ask for tea—when she heard the words, 'We leave for Jamalbad at first light tomorrow. All you need do is prepare a light breakfast and then you are free to go. You will have the day to clear your things before the house is closed up.'

They were leaving? Tomorrow? So that was why they wouldn't need a chef any longer. And if they didn't need a chef…

She stood there, drinking in the knowledge that her services were about to be terminated prematurely, and the clatter of pans coming from the kitchen as Anton grudgingly came to terms with the news echoed her mood.

She'd thought she still had two weeks of being Nobilah's companion. Now she had less than twenty-four hours. *Damn.* Working nine to five in some office hellhole was going to seem very ordinary after this assignment.

'Miss Fielding?'

Morgan blinked and swung around to see Kamil watching her from the kitchen door, a frown creasing his brow. Mentally she prepared herself, waiting for the axe to fall. Kamil had been the one to hire her. If her services were about to be terminated, he might as well get it over with right now. But he just stared right back at her.

'Was there something you wanted?'

She hesitated, still expecting him to take advantage of finding her outside the kitchen to deliver the news of her own dismissal. But when he failed to speak again, Morgan could put it off no longer. She nodded, feeling awkward. 'Nobilah requested tea.'

He looked at her oddly, his expression a mix of concern and something that looked like pity. Then he simply glanced over his shoulder. 'Anton, tea for Nobilah, if you please.' He turned back to Morgan. 'Was there anything else?'

*You tell me*, she was tempted to say. 'No,' she whispered instead. 'Just the tea.'

'In that case, please excuse me. I have much to arrange. Anton will have the tea ready for you in just a moment.' He nodded and turned to leave, but all of a sudden she couldn't let him go—not without knowing for sure.

'Kamil…'

He halted and swivelled back round. 'Yes?'

'I...I'm sorry, but I couldn't help but overhear. You're leaving for Jamalbad? Tomorrow?'

He inclined his head. 'That is true.'

'The entire household, including Nobilah?'

'Again, this is true.'

'Oh,' she whispered. 'I see.'

Kamil hesitated a moment, and once more she caught almost a look of pity in his features—but in a blink it was gone, his usual mask of efficiency returned.

'If that is all...?'

'Of course,' she said, letting him withdraw. He would have plenty to do to organise the family's early departure without her getting in his way.

Why had he looked at her that way? she wondered as she carried the tray from the kitchen. Unless Kamil had assumed she might be expecting a generous bonus for the early termination of her contract too?

He needn't be worried on that score. Anton had been with them for the best part of two months, and was a top-flight chef, while she'd been Nobilah's companion for little more than a week. Under the circumstances she'd be more than happy to have her contract paid out.

She slowed as she crossed the terrace, her pulse starting to beat irregularly as she took in the sight of Nobilah with her son. They were walking side by side along the stone flagging that lined the large, Italian-inspired pool. Tajik dwarfed his mother, a petite woman for all her curves, rendered all the more petite by the man walking alongside her and whose elegance could not be disguised by the abaya she wore, its fabric swirling about her like poetry as she walked.

And then there was Tajik. Tall and broad-shouldered and hard, as if he'd been carved from stone and breathed into life by the kiss of the gods. His pale blue sweater could not mask a firm chest and flat abdomen; his dark trousers could not disguise lean hips and long legs.

As she watched, he angled his face towards his mother, and Morgan found herself reacquainted with the determined angles of his jaw, the strong line of his nose. Everything about the man said power, even the fire-flecked golden eyes and the passionate slash of his mouth.

What did his return today have to do with the family's sudden departure? It couldn't be coincidental. There'd been no hint of a possible early return to Jamalbad before now.

Not that there was anything she could do about it. With a sigh she pushed herself off the deck, heading for the pool area while the pair were still strolling around the far end of the pool. Screened by trees, she'd take the opportunity of leaving the tea on the table and make herself scarce while mother and son enjoyed their reunion. She had no desire to lock horns—or gazes, for that matter—with Sheikh Tajik again, not when he had such a disconcerting ability to get under her skin.

Morgan gave a wry smile as she reached the table. If she had to find a bright side to the early end to this assignment, she guessed being saved any further contact with Sheik Tajik would probably fit the bill. That would be some consolation at least.

He'd known the second she'd emerged from the house. He'd felt her presence like a sigh of satisfaction. She'd taken a long time, much longer than it took to collect a mere pot of tea, and he'd wondered if he'd actually scared her off completely. After all, she'd almost bolted for the sanctuary of the house the second Nobilah had mentioned the word "tea".

He'd waited with unexpected enthusiasm for her to rejoin them while he'd gone over the plans to leave with his mother, until finally Morgan had reappeared, but even then she'd hesitated, like some quaking virgin on her way to her wedding feast—knowing but not really comprehending what was in store for her.

He allowed himself a smile at the parallel as his mother headed back to the house to check with Kamil on progress.

Morgan was perfect. Up close he could see she was both good-looking enough for everyone to believe he'd chosen her as his bride for just that reason alone, and meek enough not to complicate his plans. She was exactly what he needed to quash Qasim's lust for the throne.

He watched her place the tray on the table, her cream linen trousers moulding to her neat backside as she bent down, emphasising the flare of her hips and firing off a primitive spike of need in his loins that took him both by surprise and delight. Oh, no, he thought as he circled the pool towards her, appreciating the neat waist between those feminine curves, it would be no hardship playing Qasim at his own game. Not with such an appetizing partner in crime.

The object of his attention straightened and set off without a backward glance. He smiled to himself. She was kidding herself if she thought she could escape that easily.

'Miss Fielding,' he called. 'You will be joining me for tea.' It wasn't a question.

She stopped with a jolt, before her back straightened and she swung around.

The polite smile on her face did nothing to hide her obvious discomfiture at being caught.

'I'm afraid I only brought two cups.'

He swung his hand around in a sweeping arc that could only emphasise the leanness in his body, the sheer latent strength. 'As you can see, there are only two of us.'

'But Nobilah?' Frantically her eyes scanned the pool area.

'Has gone to organise the staff,' he finished.

She took a step towards the house. 'Then I should help her.'

'No.' His hand whipped out and caught her forearm, arresting her mid-turn. 'Not just yet. I wanted the opportunity to talk to you.'

She looked up at him, her hazel eyes wide with what looked almost like panic, her lips still parted with surprise. Underneath his hand her skin felt smooth and warm, and his thumb picked up the race of her pulse through her slender limb.

Then her chin kicked up on a swallow. 'If it's about leaving tomorrow, I already know.' She looked down at his hand. 'So, if you'll kindly take your hand away…'

He didn't. Not right away. He let it linger long enough to drink in more of the touch of her skin, long enough to tell her that *he* was the one who would decide what and where. As she would soon come to know.

Finally he let her go, and she clutched her arms around her as if she was cold. But he knew from her touch that she wasn't cold. *Far from it.*

'Walk with me,' he said, 'and tell me what you think you know.'

Her eyes sparked at the implication, but she said

nothing, merely falling into step alongside him as he set off along the path that threaded through the palms around the perimeter. She walked with a slight limp, he noticed, a limp she was working hard at disguising.

For a moment he wondered if he was acting too rashly and there might be some pressing medical reason why he would be foolish to take this woman as his wife, but if Kamil had not listed it amongst his concerns, as surely he would have, then it must be a detail of no consequence. Beside him the woman gave a small sigh of resignation.

'Just that the household is returning to Jamalbad tomorrow and that everyone will be leaving.'

'You're not sorry? I believe from Kamil that your contract has two weeks to run?'

'I will miss Nobilah.'

He nodded, liking the way this conversation was developing. 'As my mother seems to like you.'

She smiled in return, transforming her features to dazzling. 'I love hearing Nobilah's stories of life in Jamalbad. I don't know.' She shrugged. 'It just all sounds so exotic.'

She looked up at him, her eyes bright and her smile wide, until, as suddenly as if she'd flicked a switch, her eyes clouded over and she let her smile slide away.

'Anyway,' she continued, looking ahead once more, the prim miss back in control, 'I will miss her.'

He waited a stride or two before answering, taking his time to appreciate the slightly irregular sway of her hips as they walked together. It was good. Even the way she moved pleased him. 'That will not be necessary,' he told her.

He heard the rapid intake of air that preceded her words.

'Look, it may not be *necessary*, as you put it, but I do like your mother. I've enjoyed her company immensely, whether you believe me or not.'

Her sudden outburst took him by surprise. So the meek-looking girl had some spirit after all? That might be a drawback if it meant she would not fall in with his plans, but then again it might make this a more interesting exercise than he'd imagined. Right now, though, he could do without getting her off-side.

'You misunderstand me,' he soothed. 'I do not doubt your affection for my mother. I am saying merely that you will have no reason to miss her.'

'What are you saying?'

'That you are traveling to Jamalbad with us.'

'Me?'

'You are needed in Jamalbad.'

'As Nobilah's companion?'

He looked down at her. He would have to remember to thank his mother—she had made his job so much easier. 'Fatima will be at least six weeks regaining her strength following her surgery.'

'So you'll be extending my contract?'

'In a matter of speaking. I promise you it will be worth your while.'

Something about the way he said that managed to pierce the bubble of enthusiasm she'd been feeling at the news.

Jamalbad—she'd loved the very thought of the place since Nobilah had first mentioned it. The earth buildings looking as if they'd emerged fully formed from the surrounding sands, the white shell-encrusted palace walls glistening in the midday sun, the jewel colours of the women's robes. The thought of seeing it for herself had been nothing short of a dream, and now she was being offered a chance to make that dream come true. And yet something about the offer seemed almost too good to be true.

*Something didn't feel right.*

'Surely there are plenty of women in Jamalbad who could perform the role of Nobilah's companion?'

'I have no doubt of that. Would that stop you from going?'

'Well, no, but—'

'Then perhaps you have had a better offer?'

'No, it's not that.'

'Then it is settled.' He smiled. 'Come,' he said, directing her back to the table, where the tea sat waiting, 'have tea with me.'

Morgan wavered. She wasn't sure she wanted to have tea with him. Especially now she felt she was being railroaded into going to Jamalbad—which was crazy when visiting Jamalbad was something she wanted to do. But tomorrow?

She almost never acted on impulse. That was her twin sister Tegan's department. Gutsy Tegan, who'd come home from her aid work in Somalia and agreed to swap places with Morgan for a week while she attended a wedding in Fiji. Gutsy Tegan, who'd had no choice but to stay on for two months after Morgan's broken leg and surgery. Gutsy Tegan, who'd fallen in love with Morgan's boss from hell and turned him into the perfect husband.

Tegan would jump at such an opportunity, she knew. But Morgan had always been the quiet one. *The sensible one.* She hauled in a breath, only to find it tinged with the rich scent of the man beside her—sandalwood, exotic spices, musk—an alluring mix that seemed to latch into her senses and beckon to her.

But tomorrow?

'It's just not as simple as that,' she said at last.

'It's not?' he asked ingenuously, with a shrug. 'It is only tea.'

Exasperated, she slipped into a chair when it was clear he was not going to take no for an answer. Without asking he picked up the delicate teapot and, with an unexpected sensuality of movement, tilted the pot to pour tea into her cup. It was there in the curve of his fingers around the teapot. It was there in the steady pour of tea into her cup, in the heady scent of spices in the heated steam. It was there in the unwavering way he met her gaze with those golden eyes that seemed to see right inside her.

She cleared her throat, hoping it might go some way to clearing her mind. 'I didn't actually mean the tea. I'm talking about going to Jamalbad with you…I mean with Nobilah.'

'I know what you meant. But you've already said that you don't have a better offer. You yourself said you love what Nobilah has already told you about Jamalbad. I am offering you the chance to go there and see it for yourself. Why should you have any reason to turn down this opportunity?' He paused, his cup almost to that sensuous slash of mouth. 'Unless there is a man?' He shrugged. 'A boyfriend, perhaps?'

Maybe it was the earnest way he said it, but Morgan wanted to laugh out loud. Except one look at his eyes warned her not to. He was serious.

'Does Jamalbad have a problem with women who have boyfriends?'

'Would it be an issue for you if it did?'

She tried to hold his gaze, but she knew the rising heat

she could feel colouring her skin would give her away anyway. 'No,' she acknowledged with a shake of her head.

He nodded. 'That is for the best.'

She blinked. 'What's that supposed to mean?'

'Jamalbad is in a lot of ways a modern Arab emirate. However, we come from a very traditional society where women are still prized for their...shall we say, "purity"? While you are in our country, we would expect you to behave with a certain modesty.'

'You mean as opposed to jumping into bed with every man I meet?'

His cool golden gaze collided dispassionately with her own. 'I wouldn't have put it quite so coarsely myself.'

'Yet you have no problem thinking it.' She replaced her cup on her saucer. 'Well, it may just surprise you to know that there are some women in Australia who *don't* jump into bed with every guy they meet.'

'That is encouraging news. And would you count yourself in their number?'

She stood up quickly, the metal legs of her chair scraping across the sandstone tiles of the pool surrounds.

'What is this? Next you'll asking for some kind of medical certificate or something.'

'That won't be necessary,' he said, rising alongside her. 'I think you've made your point. You see, the women of the palace are easily influenced by the lure of the western life, and, while I encourage their education in most respects, there are some practices I would prefer them not to adopt.'

'Well, you have no fear on that count. They're hardly likely to learn anything from *me*.'

His golden eyes glimmered in a way that sent vibrations

dancing along her nerve-endings. Why did he look that way at her? Like a jungle cat sizing her up for the kill rather than someone who had to decide if she was morally upright enough to be invited to his country?

'I expected you to be totally docile, but you surprise me with your anger. Do you have any idea how beautiful you are when you are angry?'

His words blindsided her. Nobody had called her beautiful—not since Evan—and she couldn't believe what *he'd* said anyway. But the man opposite her was right about one thing—she was certainly angry. Morgan Fielding—who prided herself on staying cool under pressure—was cracking up. Something she'd never done even with Maverick, the boss with the worst reputation in the Gold Coast.

'Well, then,' she said, uncomfortable in the loud silence that followed, 'given that I have such a fiery temper, I wonder if I have given you yet another reason not to be considered morally upright enough to accompany Nobilah to Jamalbad?'

She tried to toss the question off lightly, to head off the mounting tension filling the air between them, but his eyes just crinkled at the edges, their golden depths deepening like warm caramel.

'On the contrary,' he murmured, his voice deep and resonant. 'You will be perfect.'

## CHAPTER THREE

TEGAN eased the sleeping baby from her breast and offered her to her twin. 'Would you like to burp her, seeing as you won't have the chance again for a while? Maverick will be home in a couple of minutes, and I just want to finish the salad.'

'Please,' Morgan said, taking the infant and propping her gently over her shoulder as she swayed from side to side, rubbing the infant's back.

After a frantic few hours helping Nobilah pack and arranging her own affairs, it was so restful to hold her new niece while standing looking out through the palms to the placid waters of the Gold Coast canal beyond. There was still plenty to organise, but Nobilah had insisted Morgan take some time to visit her sister and her family before she left. Very soon her sister's husband, Maverick, would be home, and their conversation would not be so open. Right now it was worthwhile to be able to talk sister to sister.

Baby Ellie rewarded her ministrations with a very unladylike burp. She laughed as the infant briefly nuzzled her neck before settling back into a doze. 'Oh, I'm going to miss you, little one,' she said, pressing her lips to the baby's head.

'When will you be back?' her sister asked from the spacious kitchen.

'I'm not exactly sure. A few weeks, I guess.'

Tegan looked up sharply. 'You mean you don't *know* when you're coming back? That you're being whisked away to some tiny Arab emirate and you have no idea when you're coming home?'

Morgan shrugged. 'Sheikh Tajik didn't say, but I guess it's just until Fatima recovers enough to take over her duties again. I don't expect it to be for more than a few weeks.'

Tegan opened the refrigerator, pulling out the salad dressing she'd prepared earlier.

'So what's he like, this Sheikh?'

Morgan took a deep breath, her lungs filled with the fresh scent of newborn baby, while her mind battled to get a grip on the confusing images and impressions of Sheikh Tajik. It was hard to mesh the images—the dutiful son who had taken over the leadership of his country after his father's tragic death. The man who had bossed her mercilessly by the pool and told her everything was settled before she'd even had a chance to assimilate the news of her invitation to Jamalbad. The man who'd gazed into her soul with those golden eyes and left her strangely shaken...

'I don't know,' she said at last. 'I only met him today.'

'So he's not tall, dark and handsome, then?'

This time Morgan shook her head with no hesitation at all. 'No,' she said, 'not exactly. He's tall and broad-shouldered, and his hair is dark...'

'But he's not handsome?'

Morgan wavered. "Handsome" seemed too soft a word. He was strong-featured. With eyes that saw too much and revealed nothing that didn't scare her. No, he wasn't just handsome. He was beyond handsome.

*He was disturbing.*

A tremor moved through her and she clutched tiny Eleanor to her chest to disguise it. 'Not exactly,' she replied, wishing for a change of subject.

'And is he married?'

'What's that got to do with anything?'

'You tell me,' responded Tegan with renewed interest as she arranged a couple of things on the table. 'You're the one who seems a bit affected by him.'

'Forget it,' Morgan lied. 'It's just that this is all a bit sudden. Besides, you know I'm not looking for a relationship.'

Tegan regarded her solemnly. 'But you're obviously desperate to have your own family.'

Morgan opened her mouth to defend herself, but Tegan was right there.

'Just look at the way you are with Ellie! Don't try telling me you're not getting clucky.'

'I love my niece. Isn't that normal?'

'It's not normal to be pining over a failed relationship years after the event.'

'I am not!'

Tegan gave her a searching look that left her sister in no doubt she disagreed. 'Look at yourself, Morgan. You've buried yourself in your work for years, covering yourself up like a nun—just because that idiot Evan didn't appreciate what he had.'

Morgan grunted. 'Oh, he appreciated what he had, all right. Getting engaged to me meant he could protect his

precious family from the truth about him. He used me, and
I was so stupid I fell for it.'

Tegan placed the salad on the table and came over to
wrap an arm around her sister's shoulders, giving them a
squeeze. 'Hey, you were in love with him.'

'No,' Morgan said, shaking her head. 'I thought I was.
But I was just in love with the idea of being in love—and
with the idea that someone wanted to marry me. He didn't
want me at all, except to use me. I'm never letting anyone
do that to me again.'

'Which doesn't mean you have to shut yourself off from
the entire world! You'll hardly find a man if you lock
yourself away. In fact, I'm glad you're going on this trip.
Who knows where it might lead?'

Morgan didn't answer straight away, instead thinking
that since marrying Maverick her sister had become a
hopeless romantic. She kissed the sleeping infant's hair
and laid her down in her bassinet, tucking the light blankets
in around her. Her task complete, she turned to her sister.

'I know you only want me to be as happy as you are
now, but I really think you've got the wrong idea. I'm
going to the desert for a few weeks to keep a middle-aged
woman company, nothing more. So if you think I'm going
to be coming home with any more than a toy camel, then
you're in for a big disappointment.'

After dinner Maverick offered to drive Morgan back to
the sprawling mansion that served as a holiday home for
Nobilah, stopping off along the way to let her pick up her
passport and a few odd things she wanted to collect from
her apartment, and to let her neighbours know she'd be
away for a few weeks.

It was late by the time Maverick steered the car through

the gates and pulled up outside the mansion that stood silent and imposing under the bright moonlight.

'Thanks for the lift,' she said, keeping her voice low as he hauled her bag from the boot and swung it down onto the paving alongside her. 'You take care of my little sister and Ellie.'

'You know I will,' he replied, placing one hand on her shoulder. 'But who's going to take care of you? Tegan's worried about you going off with no idea of when you'll be back.'

'Don't you start,' she said, wishing everyone would stop mirroring the very misgivings she was having. It was one thing to head off to Jamalbad to accompany Nobilah. It was another thing entirely to know that Sheikh Tajik, with his golden eyes and unsettling presence, was going to be part of the package. 'I'll be fine,' she said, as much to convince herself as anything, and she stretched up to give her brother-in-law a hug and a heartfelt kiss on the cheek.

His long arms enclosed her and he gave her a mighty squeeze that lifted her feet from the ground before, with a final kiss and saying, 'Take care,' he was back behind the wheel.

Morgan waited while he drove away, one hand lifted in a silent farewell. She didn't know how long she would be away, but she knew she would miss her Gold Coast family and her new niece. Then the car turned onto the road and disappeared from view, and the fingers of her open hand curled as a prickling sensation needled its way down her spine. This was it, the point of no return, and that realisation sent excitement vying with a menacing anxiety inside her. But she'd told Maverick she'd be fine. She'd better start believing it, given she'd be on the plane in less than eight hours.

With a sigh, she bent down to pick up her bag. It was whipped out of her reach from behind. She gasped and reeled around, only to find a mountain standing between her and the door.

'Where have you been all this time?'

'You startled me,' she managed to say, her hand covering a thumping heart she knew would never completely settle back to normal—not while she was in this man's presence. 'I can carry my own luggage, thank you.' She held out her hand to take the bag, but he ignored it.

'Why are you so late?'

Shock turned to indignation. 'I didn't realise you were going to wait up for me. What an honour.'

She regretted the jibe the moment it had left her mouth—*what was it about this man that brought out the worst in her?*—but he merely brushed it aside by slashing his free hand in the direction of the departed vehicle. 'Who was the man you were whispering to? That you were kissing?'

'Why, Sheikh Tajik,' she purred, with more bravado than she had ever known, 'I didn't realise you cared.' Then she attempted to coolly brush past the looming mountain in her path, knowing that if he could hear the blood thumping in her veins he would know she was anything but cool.

But his hand shot out and circled her wrist before she could pass, trapping her alongside the long, hard length of him. 'You told me you had no boyfriends.'

'And you think I lied? Shame on you for your lack of trust.'

'Then who was he?'

'What possible business can it be of yours?'

'Tell me!'

Her chest heaving, she glared up at him, not missing the way fury had tightened the skin covering his features and turned the tendons in his throat to steel pillars. 'It was my brother-in-law! My very happily married brother-in-law, I might add. There,' she said, as her news sank in, sweet satisfaction dripping from her voice, 'are you satisfied now?'

The ragged sound of his breathing was his only response—that and the turmoil in his golden eyes, filling the silence with an atmosphere more threatening than any words.

She gasped and tried to pull away, but his grip was made of iron, his hold relentless.

'Why did you not tell me you were going out?'

She twisted her arm, still fruitlessly trying to free herself. 'Your mother knew. Why didn't you ask her?'

'Nobilah is in bed.'

'Which is exactly where I intend to be, once you deign to let me go!'

Silence followed her outburst. Silence heavy with a new kind of tension. *Heavy with desire.* She could sense it thickening the air between them. She could see it in the set of his jaw and the glimmer of his eyes. Once more she cursed herself for her ill-chosen words.

'Now, there's an idea,' he said, in little more than a growl, sending tremors skittering up her spine anew.

In the instant before it happened she saw it coming. Which meant she had less than an instant to act to prevent it.

And yet she did nothing, mesmerised by the alluring touch of his fingers angling her chin higher, by the deeply seductive lure of his mouth as it dipped to meet hers.

And then his lips touched hers and she knew she'd waited too long to stop him. She tried to tell herself she cared. And she would care later, she knew. But for now she was content to drink in the power in the coaxing caress of his lips, to feel his desire like the gentle hiss of the ocean pulling back before the next inevitable wave crashed in.

His mouth moved over hers. Intoxicating. Seductive. And if he picked up on her inexperience, he didn't let on. But then, he made it easy to follow his lead—just as he made it impossible not to want to. Not when he tasted of power and strength and all things exotic, an intoxicating mix that had her melting against him.

There was a sound—her bag hitting the tiled floor—before she felt herself enclosed in his embrace, his strong arms moulding her to him length to length, his hands holding her tight, and suddenly it wasn't just her mouth and lips involved in this kiss, it was every part of her. She could barely think. She could hardly breathe. And what oxygen there was seemed only to fuel the blast furnace of their kiss.

And then, before she could assimilate all the sensations, before she could make sense of what was happening, it was over.

His head pulled back, his arms slid away, leaving her trembling like an adolescent who'd just had her first kiss.

And realisation dawned on her like a cloud-filled morning. If Tajik had been looking for an excuse to leave her behind, a reason to doubt her lack of sexual experience, she'd just handed it to him on a platter.

Desperately she searched for some of her earlier bravado. She wiped her mouth with the back of her hand, wishing she could wipe the entire experience away as easily. 'What the hell was that for?' she said, trying to quell the shaking in her voice.

He looked down at her, all golden power and dark desire, his breathing heavy. 'I told you that you were beautiful when you were angry,' he said, his voice little more than a coarse rumble that tugged at her raw nerve-endings and refused to let them settle. 'But it is nothing to how beautiful you are when you are aroused.'

'Oh, n…no,' she stammered, shaking her head as she took a wobbly step back. 'I was hardly—' But she couldn't bring herself to say the word. By saying it she would be admitting it, and by admitting it when she was about to board a plane with him for Jamalbad, for goodness knew how long, she would be in real trouble.

'So you always kiss men like that when you are not aroused?'

'I don't kiss men like that—period! You just took me by surprise.'

His eyes proclaimed a victory that made no sense to her. How could it be victory when he hadn't won that kiss? She'd damn near volunteered it. And why that didn't have him terminating her contract on the spot, when he'd been so insistent on her virtue before, made even less sense.

'By surprise, you say? And I say you are proving to be a more delightful surprise by the minute.'

'And you are proving to be more irritating by the minute!'

For a moment he looked too shocked to respond. She was wondering if she'd well and truly overstepped the mark— here was a man used to people kow-towing to him, a man who could put paid to any idea of her entering his country— when he suddenly threw back his head and laughed.

It was too much. Indignation lent strength to her backbone. She reached down and grabbed her bag. She needed to be in her room.

No, it was much simpler than that. She needed to be anywhere he wasn't. She reached for the door handle and turned it.

The laughter stopped behind her just as suddenly as it had started. 'Miss Fielding.'

His voice rang out like an order. Her hand paused and reluctantly she looked over her shoulder, half wishing she was more like her sister. Giving anyone lip had never been Morgan's forte. Why had she ever expected to go head to head with a man like this and get away with it?

She took one look into his eyes, shocked at what she saw. Under the night sky he could have been some kind of jungle cat, golden eyes glistening with hunger and the guarantee of a certain kill. She shivered, her heart thumping afresh, certain that he was about to terminate her services, if not her.

'What is it?' she whispered, her voice little more than a shudder.

'We leave at six,' he said. 'Be ready.'

The sleek jet crouched low on the tarmac, its El Jamal insignia curling artistically up the tail, whilst heated air from the warming engines turned the landscape behind into a shimmer. Inside the limousine speeding out over the tarmac towards it, Morgan knew her thoughts had just as little clarity.

Her fuzzy head was only partly to blame—it had taken her hours to get to sleep, and when she had her tortured dreams of a dark and dangerous pursuer had left her tangled in the sheets. She should never have let Tajik kiss her. She should have pushed him away.

And then the car slowed, and the real reason for both her sleepless night and her muddled thoughts caught her eye and held on tight. Oh, no, she thought, as she felt herself drowning in those liquid eyes. It wasn't just the kiss and what she should have done. The real reason for her addled brain was the man who sprawled so nonchalantly opposite her, his long legs eating up the space between them, his hands steepled over his stomach as his eyes lazily contemplated her.

And as he watched her lips tingled with the memories of that kiss, with the warm press of his lips and the welcoming sensuality of his mouth. She bit down on her own betraying lips and turned away as the car came to a halt.

Beside her Nobilah squeezed her hand, misinterpreting Morgan's lack of enthusiasm. 'Don't be nervous. Our pilots are the best in the world,' she said with a smile in her son's direction. 'And by tonight we'll be there. You're going to love Jamalbad.'

Morgan didn't doubt it. But she knew she'd like it one heck of a lot better if Tajik wasn't part of the deal. She smiled back, fully aware of the Sheikh's continued scrutiny. 'I know I will.'

Then the door was pulled open, and it was time to alight and board the streamlined jet.

'Goodbye, Gold Coast,' Morgan muttered as she followed Nobilah up the stairs into the plane, taking her last look back at the familiar shape of Tamborine Mountain and the range that bordered the Gold Coast strip and marked the start of the hinterland.

Her words were whipped away by the wind that tugged

at her fitted skirt and tightly knotted hair, but still she paused at the top of the stairs, hesitant to take that final step into the plane.

'What's wrong?' asked the Sheikh, bounding up the stairs two at a time behind her. 'Fear of flying?'

She looked back at him, his linen pants and white shirt emphasising his dark hair and framing his golden good looks, and she felt her world of security and planning start to crumble.

How could a man look both cool and hot at the same time? How could he have eyes that looked coldly assessing one minute, yet rich with molten desire the next?

And how could she feel both fear and yet such a bewildering attraction? What was it about this man that unsettled her on so many levels?

She shook her head, more to clear her thoughts than to answer his question, but it served the purpose. 'I'm just not too good with turbulence,' she answered honestly. *Not since the accident.*

'In that case,' he said, climbing a step higher so that his eyes were on the same level and just inches from her own, 'let's hope this is all plain sailing.'

Was he talking about the flight? As she searched his eyes all she could think about was another time when his face had been so close, his lips just a heartbeat from hers. Her gaze dropped to those lips, her pulse kicking up as she remembered the sensual press of them against her own, the masterful way he'd overcome her initial resistance, the easy way he'd melted her from the inside out.

Then those lips turned into a smile that broke into her thoughts, forcing her eyes back to his.

'I know,' he said, his voice a clear and steady thread

amid the noise of screaming engines. 'I keep thinking about it too.'

Did he mean what she thought he meant? Were her thoughts so obvious?

It took a few moments to find her voice, given the tremors that coursed through her body. 'I don't know what you mean.' Then she turned and headed into the plane, knowing full well that it hadn't been fear of flying that had held up her progress boarding. It was knowing that once inside she would no longer be in her world.

*She would be in his.*

Tajik watched her enter the plane, enjoying her discomfiture almost as much as he'd enjoyed last night's kiss. That had been a surprise—the urgency of his passion like a beast demanding to be fed. But it was little wonder, he mused as he moved towards the cockpit. It had been a long time since he'd had a woman, after all, and this one promised to deliver everything he would need from her in that department. She'd shocked herself too with the force of her response, if her eyes had been any indication.

Visions of another pair of eyes, deeply expressive and framed with kohl, intruded on his thoughts, and once again he felt a stab of guilt that he might feel an attraction to another woman—and one so different from his fiancée. But what choice did he have? Joharah was gone, and reports overnight had only confirmed what Kamil had discovered. Taj needed to take a wife, and soon, if he was to put paid to his cousin's moves to angle the sheikhdom under his control.

He greeted the other pilot and strapped himself into his seat, his mind exploring every memory and nuance of that kiss.

Besides, he told himself as he picked up the flight charts

to look them over, if he had to marry anyone, and convince
Qasim that it was a real marriage, then it was far better for
there to be some kind of attraction between them.

*And there was definitely that.*

## CHAPTER FOUR

THE interior of the plane was nothing like she'd ever seen before. Morgan was used to commercial airlines, with their row upon row of close-fitting seats and vinyl everything, but after being guided to the right through a short passage, she saw the cabin opened into what looked more like a lounge room, with a scattering of armchairs and tables sprinkled around the sides of the jet. Richly patterned carpet adorned the floor, and artworks lined the polished walnut walls. And from the glimpse she'd had, the rest of the plane's interior was divided into more rooms beyond.

The dark-eyed flight attendant showed her to a plush leather chair, alongside which Nobilah was already enjoying a pre-flight glass of juice. Tajik, she noticed, had vanished.

She buckled her seatbelt and accepted the glass of juice that had arrived unbidden. 'You mentioned that we'd be there tonight,' she said to the older woman. 'How long is the flight?'

'Around fourteen to fifteen hours. I'm afraid there's not much to do but read or watch movies until then.'

'Sounds terrible,' joked Morgan, finally starting to recover now that Tajik wasn't around to throw her into a spin.

'Where are the others?' she asked a little while later, curiosity getting the better of her as Tajik failed to appear. 'Kamil and Sheikh Tajik.'

'Kamil will no doubt be in his office, sorting out the paperwork.' Nobilah pointed to a narrow cabin they'd passed on the way in. 'And Taj will be in the cockpit.'

'He's flying the plane?'

Nobilah laughed and patted Morgan's hand. 'Don't look so alarmed. Taj is an excellent pilot. Now, what film do you think we should watch first?'

Morgan offered her opinion, and then settled back into her comfortable chair for the takeoff. If Tajik was busy in the cockpit, rather than here in the lounge, then maybe this flight wouldn't be the ordeal she'd imagined. And, given he'd left her with not a word, maybe she'd read too much into that moment on the stairs.

*As maybe she'd read far too much into that kiss.*

Yes, he was attractive and charismatic, and he had a way of looking at her that made her heart lurch to a standstill, but he was the ruler of an independent Arab country. Way beyond anything in her experience. Way out of her league.

He'd be well used to escorting the world's most beautiful women to the world's most beautiful places. And no doubt he was equally at home making love to them. In which case that stolen kiss last night in a dimly lit gateway probably didn't even register with him. Beyond making a point of how morally suspect she was, of course.

But then why had he told her that he kept thinking about it too? Unless he was reminding her of how easy she'd seemed?

Morgan squeezed her eyes shut and pinched the bridge of her nose. It was only yesterday she'd first met Sheikh Tajik. And it was only yesterday she'd learned of her sudden trip to Jamalbad. No wonder her nerves were frayed. She needed to unwind and get things back into perspective. She might as well enjoy the flight, and then, once back in Jamalbad, he'd be busy ruling his sheikhdom, or whatever it was that sheikhs did, while she'd no doubt be ensconced in the women's quarters with Nobilah. She'd probably hardly ever see him.

Which suited her just fine.

A few minutes later the plane powered down the runway and speared into the sky, pushing them back in their seats. Morgan watched the Queensland coastline shrink as the plane wheeled around, heading inland and tracking northwest. All too soon the colours of the land below changed from the green coastal fringe to the endless red of the Australian interior, until cloud cover reduced the view to nothing more than a mattress of cotton wool at the bottom of a clear blue sky, and Morgan transferred her attention to the romantic comedy Nobilah had selected.

Luxury could make a long trip bearable, Morgan decided a few hours later, as she worked with Nobilah on a crossword. She'd discovered that the wide chairs converted into recliners, and the flight attendant had ensured that their every need was anticipated. The sparkling water by her side was kept topped up, and snacks of dried figs and nuts appeared like magic. If she'd asked for anything else it would have been delivered in a flash and with a smile, as if it was her God-given right.

Flying gold class, she thought, had its advantages. Although it was more like platinum class, she corrected, as she glanced around at her luxurious surroundings. It was hard to believe she was on a plane thirty-five thousand feet above the earth. It was harder to believe she somehow deserved such special treatment. It was certainly a change from when she'd returned home from Fiji with her leg in plaster a few short months ago, and had had to be wheeled on and off a normal commercial jetliner.

Morgan stretched out that leg now, pointing her toes and making circles with her ankle. There was just a twinge, like a memory of pain long gone, but apart from that her leg felt almost as good as new. It would never be perfect, the doctors had warned her—she'd sustained too many fractures and too much trauma for that—but for a normal life with no thrill-seeking or endurance sports involved it would be fine. Morgan had laughed when the doctors had made that pronouncement—there was absolutely no chance of that!

Just when she thought the flight couldn't get any more sumptuous, they were invited to lunch in the dining room, and once again Morgan felt her eyes open wide at the sight. It was a room as large as the lounge, with a massive table at least three metres long and a metre wide, the tabletop cut from one single magnificent slab of timber. But it was the sight and scent of the numerous small dishes on the tasselled table runner that drew Morgan closer.

Spiced lamb, saffron rice studded with almonds and sultanas, warm flat bread and a myriad other colourful dishes worked their magic and drew her to the table like a magnet. Suddenly the hours since breakfast made themselves felt, and her stomach protested with a loud rumble.

'I'm so hungry,' she admitted, with a hand over her stomach.

Nobilah laughed. 'Then you've come to the right place. Take a seat.'

The food was every bit as good as it looked. And filling.

Fifteen minutes later Morgan wasn't hungry any more. She sipped on mineral water while Nobilah finished her meal, and a series of portraits along the wall caught her attention. She recognised a photograph of Sheikh Tajik at the end of the line-up.

She excused herself to take a closer look, drifting past them all until she came to the one that had caught her eye. Like all the others, the man was wearing traditional white robes and a headpiece, and as his angled gaze stared regally off into the distance he looked every part the warrior king. She could just imagine him sitting astride a horse atop a desert dune, reins in one hand, a rifle in the other. King of the desert.

'Do you see the resemblance?'

She turned. She'd been so deep in thought she hadn't even heard Nobilah join her. 'This is Ashraf,' she said, gesturing towards the penultimate portrait. 'Tajik's father and my husband.'

'It's a strong resemblance,' Morgan conceded. 'But I think you've given him your eyes. They're such an unusual colour—almost gold in some light.'

Nobilah smiled. 'They're very much like my father's were. It's a family trait. But he has Ashraf's fine looks otherwise. Sometimes I can almost imagine it's him…' Her last words were said on a sigh as she gazed wistfully at the picture, before shaking her head and touching a tissue to her eyes. 'Please forgive me. It's been a year since he left us.'

Morgan heard the hurt in the older woman's words, noticed the clouds form in her eyes, and turned her attention to the portrait. The man looked out from the photo proud and strong, and it was easy to discern the noble features he'd bestowed upon his son—the same strong jaw and nose, the same bearing.

'What happened to him?' she ventured, hoping she wasn't opening old wounds.

Beside her, the older woman sighed. 'Their helicopter went down…' She trailed off.

'Their?'

Nobilah turned to her, placing a hand on her forearm, a look of intense sadness in her eyes. 'He was travelling with Joharah, Tajik's fiancée, and her father.' She shook her head. 'They all died. It was a terrible, terrible time.'

Morgan wrapped an arm around the older woman's shoulders. 'It must have been,' she said, as another piece in the puzzle that was Taj slipped into place. He'd lost his father and his fiancée and inherited the sheikhdom all at the same time. What a massive load to bear.

Oh,' Nobilah said beside her. 'And this is Qasim, Ashraf's cousin. You'll meet him when we land. He's been looking after things in Jamalbad while Taj has been travelling.'

He looked nothing like his cousin, Morgan decided as she studied the picture. Deep lines divided his cheeks from his mouth, his nose hung low over a moustache and compressed lips, and his hooded eyes gazed darkly at some unseen target. No, she wasn't looking forward to meeting him.

Nobilah reeled off a few more names and stories before she yawned and put a hand to her face. 'Oh, my dear, you must excuse me. I'm going to have a nap in my room so I'm not too tired when we arrive in Jamalbad.'

'You have a room?' Morgan had thought the recliner chairs comfortable enough to sleep on, but then a private jetliner like this was bound to have its own sleeping compartments.

'There are two staterooms. Why don't you take advantage of the other one?'

'The chairs in the lounge are fine—'

'Nonsense. There's a perfectly good bed going to waste. You might as well use it. And it helps the time pass. We've still got hours to go.'

She let Nobilah lead her towards the back of the plane, past a lavishly tiled and fitted out bathroom and shower, to the two rear rooms. 'This one I prefer to use,' Nobilah said, indicating the room on their right, decorated in rich jewel shades amid gold and polished timber. 'And this one—' she pulled open a sliding door '—you are welcome to.'

Morgan stepped into the room, the masculine beauty of its glossy timbered walls and gold fittings taking her breath away. 'This must be the Sheikh's room,' she said, looking around. 'I don't think I should be here.'

'Why not? Taj isn't using it.'

Nobilah had a point. Morgan looked at the seemingly endless expanse of bed. King-sized, and covered with a glorious golden coverlet and tasselled cushions and pillows, it looked like an invitation. All of a sudden the events of the last twenty-four hours—the impact of meeting Tajik, the stress of packing up and leaving for Jamalbad within a day, the kiss Tajik had inflicted upon her last night, robbing her of hours of precious sleep—all caught up with her. Her bones were set to melting point.

Blessed sleep would be welcome. And, with Tajik an entire plane length away, he'd never know she borrowed his room.

'Thank you,' she told the other woman before she slipped away into her own room. 'I think this is a good idea after all.'

She didn't bother to get undressed, merely pulled back the cover, kicked off her shoes and slipped beneath. She wouldn't stay long. She'd just grab forty winks...

'Someone's been sleeping in my bed,' he muttered low under his breath, so not to disturb his sleeping visitor. 'And, lucky for me, she's still here.'

Tajik silently slid the door closed behind him while gazing down at her, drinking in the view. For someone who looked so buttoned up when she was awake, she seemed to sleep with wild abandon—her arms thrown out wide, her hair escaping in snaking tendrils from its tight clasp, the coverlet pushed down to her waist, revealing a tantalising sliver of skin where her shirt had come loose from her skirt.

Smooth skin, that gleamed in the low light so much like the lustre of a pearl that he wanted to reach out and run his fingers over it, to see if it felt as perfect as it looked. He felt himself stir. What a shame she hadn't got undressed before slipping under the covers.

He dragged in air and let it out on a long breath. Then again, maybe it was just as well she was dressed, otherwise he might be tempted to take her here and now. And soon enough she would be his. Soon enough he would possess her. All he had to do was bide his time and treat her gently and she would fall in with his plans without a struggle.

*And then he would have her.*

Silently he let himself through the bifold doors that led to the *en suite* bathroom attached, before peeling off his clothes and stepping into the shower.

The bus was too close to the edge—way too close for Morgan's liking—as it bumped and lurched its way along the narrow mountain track. Bend after bend she'd held her breath, while the others continued to sing and joke, as the bus swayed and tilted, somehow managing to right itself before the next tight corner. But that didn't ease the constant nausea, the constant fear that on the next corner they might not be so lucky. Nothing could. Cold sweat was her unvarying companion as the bus continued to buck and bump down the track. Cold sweat and a gut threatening to revolt.

She gripped the metal railing of the seat in front of her all the harder. The sooner they were down this mountain track the better.

Another blind bend loomed before them, and she'd already braced herself when she saw them—the twin headlights of a truck coming the other way. And there was no time to stop.

Their driver yanked the wheel to the right, while the other driver pulled in closer to the side of the mountain. The bus lurched sideways, and suddenly the laughter stopped as everyone on the bus collectively held their breath. For a second it seemed the truck would somehow miraculously squeeze past them on the inside, while their bus tilted, its tyres clinging perilously close to the edge. And then, just as the driver tried to right the bus, it happened. The slide to the right, only a matter of inches, as the right front tyre lost purchase.

People cried out to the driver. Someone screamed. The driver gunned the engine but it was fruitless. The bus refused to co-operate, no matter how much the driver cursed in his own language, urging the vehicle to climb back onto the track. The bus seemed to hang there for a moment, clinging to the side of the hill, tilted at a crazy angle, before it began its slow, unavoidable pitch over the side.

Panic overtook her. Then the crunching tumble into blackness. Then the pain that brought her back to the sound of her own screaming…

'I've got you,' someone said.

Still the bus bucked and lurched. How could anyone have her when she couldn't get a grip on herself? When her leg felt as if it was in pieces? She couldn't open her eyes, couldn't look at it, knowing it was nothing more than a mangled mess.

'I've got you,' she heard again. And this time she could feel them—the strong bands that surrounded her, bands that felt like an anchor—and her fisted hands relaxed their iron grip enough to reach out and grab hold of the security that was offered.

'It's just turbulence,' the voice said. 'The pilot is taking us higher, where it's smoother.'

*Turbulence?*

Through the fog in her head she knew something wasn't right, but when she opened her eyes it was dark and she was confused. The bumps were easing, but it wasn't the sound of cries and calls for help that met her ears, and it wasn't the smell of diesel fuel and the metallic tang of blood that filled her nose—it was the hum of engines and the calm but steady beat of a heart close to hers. It was the enticing scent of sandalwood and clean masculine skin. Clean skin of the naked chest she had wrapped herself around and was clinging to as if nothing else mattered.

And she remembered where she was in the same thunderclap that made her realise just who held her.

'Just relax,' he told her, even as her muscles tensed and contracted. 'It's okay now.'

'I'm sorry,' she whispered, trying to shrink away, her

pulse now thundering for an entirely different reason as her eyes grew more accustomed to the light—and were able to discern that it wasn't merely his chest that was bare. Legs curled beneath him. Naked legs. And a towel that looked way too small and set to pull apart with the slightest provocation. She didn't want to think about how little he might be wearing underneath—if anything. 'You can let me go now.'

If he heard her, he didn't acquiesce, merely shifted his hold on her so one arm circled her waist. The other tilted her head up towards his. 'That was some fright,' Tajik said. 'Tell me that wasn't just about the turbulence.'

She swallowed. His eyes seemed unnaturally bright, like cat's eyes glowing in the semi darkness. 'I had a bad dream. That's all.'

Morgan shivered again as memories of the panic she'd felt as the bus tumbled down the hillside washed through her. He held her till she stopped trembling, and still he wouldn't let go. Instead, his hand traced the line of her brow, brushing strands of damp hair from her face. 'You're so hot,' he told her, his fingers trailing down her face to the back of her head.

With a deftness she hadn't expected he released the clasp holding her hair tight behind her head.

'There,' he said, as he raked out the waves in her hair with his fingers, 'that should feel better.'

It did. But before she had the chance to appreciate it, his fingers dropped from her hair to her neckline. She jumped when he touched his fingers to the top button at her neck, her hand reaching up to pull his away.

Her fingers curled around his too late to stop the button's inexorable slide through its buttonhole, and his hand was already dipping to the next.

'What are you doing?' she asked, her voice little more than a breathless gasp.

'You need air,' he said, as the next button popped through. 'You're done up tighter than a drum.'

Her efforts were less than useless. Her hand was wrapped around his, but she lacked the strength to pull him away. Instead she was hypnotised by the seductive pressure of his fingers as he worked away at the button. It was strange touching him this way, feeling his fingers work under hers, feeling the strength in his large warm hand.

'That's better,' he told her, when the first four buttons were undone and he'd pulled the shirt away from her neck, stroking the skin underneath. 'Don't you agree?'

He was right. She could breathe. Or she might have been able to if only wasn't so close, *so hot*. 'I should go,' she said, trying to ignore the tremors of pleasure that moved through her every time his fingers touched her skin even while she battled to angle herself for escape over the far side of the bed. 'This is your room. I'm sorry.'

'Don't be. I wasn't using it.'

'But now…You need…' Her heart skipped a beat with a new and uncomfortable stab of panic. 'Oh God, please tell me there's someone in the cockpit.'

He smiled, softening his autocratic features and transforming them in the low light into something approximating heart-melting. 'The pilot—ably assisted by Kamil.'

'I thought *you* were flying the plane.'

He shook his head. 'Not today. Today I am merely co-pilot.'

'And Kamil can fly too?'

'Every member of my staff is qualified to undertake at least two roles. I insist on it.'

'I was only employed for one.'

'*Every* member of my staff,' he said, his voice as smooth as the darkest silk. 'I'm sure there's something else we can find for you to do.'

Her mouth was desert-dry as every bit of moisture in her body headed south. Surely he didn't mean…? But the stroke of his fingers under the hem of her shirt—*when had his hand dipped there?*—and the look in his eyes told her he was going to kiss her again if she didn't make a move right now.

'You should get dressed. And I should go.' She hesitated. 'Maybe the other way around.'

He smiled. 'Does my body worry you?'

"Worry" wasn't the word. All that gleaming satin-finished flesh, glowing in the half-light. Tempting. 'Sheikh Tajik—'

'Call me Taj.'

'Taj,' she tried, tasting his name on her tongue, thinking it sounded far too informal. *Far too intimate.*

'And I will call you Murjanah.'

She looked at him quizzically. 'What's wrong with my name?'

He touched a hand to her hair, playing the ends over his fingers. 'Murjanah is softer, I think, and more feminine. In Arabic it means "small pearl". It suits you. Because I believe that when I found you I found a small pearl indeed.'

Her mouth opened twice before she found words to fill it with. 'I should be going. Nobilah is probably waiting for me.'

'Nobilah will sleep till we are ready to land.'

'I…I shouldn't be here.'

He touched his free hand to her cheek. 'But I won't let you go.'

He had to be kidding. He was planning on keeping her here? In his bed? She pulled her arms in close to her chest, trying to look more indignant than she felt, propped up in his bed with him wearing nothing more than a towel and a predatory smile. 'You can't mean that?'

'Not until you tell me why you screamed.'

So they were back to that. She shivered as memories of the nightmare washed over her. 'It was just the turbulence…'

'You said you'd had a bad dream.'

'I know. I thought…' She closed her eyes and bowed her head.

People all around her had been groaning, calling out for help or, worse still, not moving at all. It had seemed an eternity before someone had clambered down from the truck to check on them and secure a line. It had seemed an eternity longer before medical help had arrived. It had been a miracle nobody had died. The bus's fall had been broken by a thick buffer of jungle vegetation without which they would all have plunged to their deaths down the side of the mountain.

'What did you think?'

She opened her eyes and looked up at him, yet seeing straight through him. 'It happened in Fiji last year. We'd been to see the mountain villages. The road was steep and bumpy and I was scared—we were going too fast, I thought, but we were late back to our hotel…' She let her words trail off, reluctant to commit that bus to falling one more time.

'There was an accident?' he prompted, still stroking the skin at her waist. In some respects it was like a balm, soothing and gentle. In others she feared it could only result in yet another crisis as heat crackled under his fingers, sending arrows of warmth deep, deep down. Either way, she couldn't bring herself to stop him.

'A truck met us on a blind corner. We went over the edge.'

'You were hurt?'

She nodded. 'My leg was shattered. It took the doctors hours to put it back together again. I was stuck in hospital for weeks, until it was strong enough for me to go home.'

He looked down to where the coverlet hid her legs. 'Which leg?'

She pointed to her left. 'Does it still hurt?' he asked her.

'Sometimes. It's much better now, but I have to be careful not to do anything silly.'

He reached down a hand and placed it on the cover, over her leg. She flinched instinctively from his touch, but if he noticed he didn't make any concession, just ran his hand down to where her knee lay hidden and back again. It was hardly an intimate gesture, but to Morgan it set every cell between her toes and her brain to red alert and her thighs to tingling awareness. 'In that case,' he said, 'we'll just have to make sure you don't do anything silly.'

He gave her leg one last pat before, to her relief, he took his hand away. 'So is that why you were seeking work through a temp agency? Kamil told me you came more highly qualified than the usual applicants.'

She looked up at him. Kamil had told him that? It was her turn to frown. 'Yes. I couldn't go back to my old job, and it was better that I worked casually. Then, if it was too much, I could rest in between appointments.'

'Your old boss wouldn't take you back?'

She allowed herself a smile for the first time in what seemed like for ever. 'It wasn't that simple. My sister married my boss.'

'The man I saw you with last night? The man who kissed you?'

*Right before you kissed me*, she thought, but she just nodded. 'That was Maverick—my ex-boss.'

'And he married your sister. How could that happen when you were the one who worked with him day after day?'

Her mind crunched to a halt. Was that meant to be some kind of compliment? Or was she reading way too much into things? 'It's a long story.'

'And I thought he was your boyfriend.'

She tried to laugh, but the sound came out all wrong and she resorted to words instead. 'You make it sound like you were jealous.'

'Is that so crazy?' he asked, tucking a stray tendril of hair behind her ear. 'There is something about you that draws me like a bee to the pollen.'

Her eyelids fell shut while her insides performed a rapid roll. He had to be kidding. And, even if he wasn't, she was way out of her comfort zone here. He was a sheikh, the ruler of an independent Arab country. And she was nothing more than an employee, a minor distraction during their flight. 'I really ought to be going. Thank you for…you know.'

'You feel it too, don't you?'

'Feel what?' she asked ingenuously, while every cell in her body wanted to scream *yes!*

Tajik smiled again, his fingers making lazy circles on the inside of her forearm, sending vibrations humming through every part of her and triggering a wave of further reactions—a catch in her breath, the firming of her breasts just inches from his hand, an unaccustomed ache between her thighs…

'What happens when you throw a pebble into a pond?'

His words broke into her psyche, sending her thoughts

into disarray, scattered and confused. 'There's a splash, and then ripples.'

'Exactly. A circle of ripples that expands further and further.'

The gentle pressure continued on her arm. Calming. Evocative. 'I don't understand. What does that have to do with anything?'

'Those are like the ripples I see coursing through you, when I touch you. Like the fall of a pebble into a pond, sending waves far beyond where I touch.'

Electricity shimmied up her spine. On the stairs, before they'd embarked, she'd got the impression he could read her mind. Now he was telling her he could read her body.

She shifted, searching for escape from a bed that suddenly seemed to go for ever. They'd left the turbulence long behind. There was no need for him to continue to hold her 'Sheikh—I mean Taj, I shouldn't be here. And you shouldn't say that. It's not true.'

'Prove it is not true.'

'There's no point—'

'Kiss me.'

She blinked, not sure she'd heard him right. 'Excuse me?'

'Kiss me,' he repeated, 'and tell me that you feel nothing.'

'I don't think—'

'That wasn't a request,' he murmured, his lips coming closer as his arms gathered her against his chest. 'That was an order from the Sheikh who rules over everything in Jamalbad and all its chattels. Which includes this plane and everyone on board.'

'You're telling me you're ordering me to kiss you?'

The corners of lips turned up, even as they came ever closer to hers. 'If that's what it takes.'

He couldn't do that. He couldn't insist that she kiss him. It was wrong. It was way too much too ask. Yet at the same time she felt herself fighting the fizz of excitement that came from thinking such a powerful man *wanted* her to kiss him. Was *insisting* that she kiss him.

'It doesn't work that way,' she protested, in a rare moment of rebellion, while battling to suppress the thrill that refused to be suppressed. 'You can't expect me to kiss you simply because you demand it.'

His lips—too close, too inviting—turned up into a smile. 'Then kiss me because you want to.'

Morgan had half wrenched her head away when his arm brought her back, and suddenly her choice was stolen clean away, with the seductive, warm caress of his lips on hers.

She gasped into his mouth at his audacity. She gasped at the sheer exquisite pleasure of their lips meeting. And something inside her melted. She had known it would be like this. She had feared it. He tasted of power and riches and a world of which she was no part—and yet his kiss was so welcoming as to make her feel, to make her believe, that they could be equals.

So she kissed him back. She touched a hand to his bare shoulder, telling herself she needed something to fix herself to when in truth she knew she could not help but reach out and touch that rich golden skin. Her fingers drank him in, exploring as his mouth moved over hers, undertaking their own comprehensive exploration. Smooth and warm, firm and sculpted as if from marble. Perfect.

He dipped his mouth to trail kisses down her neck, sucking, nibbling, laving her with his tongue. And this time she had no choice but to link both arms behind his neck for fear she would dissolve clean away. He moved his mouth lower, nuzzling the open skin where he'd undone her shirt at the same time as one hand worked her shirt higher, forcing her breasts to aching fullness and her back to arch involuntarily.

'So beautiful, my small pearl,' he murmured, so close against her skin that she felt his words as vibrations that fed into her very being. Then his mouth found hers again, and she felt herself being lowered to the pillows beneath him. For the first time a stab of panic interrupted the rush of pleasure.

'Sheikh Tajik—' she began.

'Taj,' he corrected instantly, claiming her mouth once more, his hand circling her ribs, his thumb stroking the underswell of her breast.

'Taj—'

Again he cut her off, this time by placing one finger over her lips. He looked down at her, his eyes speaking of a pure, unadulterated desire that threatened to undo her new-found resolve. 'Are you going to tell me you feel nothing, when I can feel you trembling in my arms even now?'

'How can I?' she answered honestly, cursing the telltale tremor that found its way even into her voice. 'But don't you think you've made your point?'

He smiled, and something else moved across his eyes— something she couldn't pin down. 'Is that what you thought I was doing—making a point?'

'Weren't you?' She took advantage of his distance and pushed herself up from the pillows, swinging her legs away from him.

A hand landed on her shoulder. 'Stay,' he urged. 'Let us finish what we have started. Make love with me, Murjanah.'

It wasn't just the words he said but the way he said them. The way his name for her rolled like foreign poetry off his tongue. Tingles bloomed throughout her body, forcing her retreating muscles to a halt. 'You don't mean that,' she said, her gaze focused on the edge of the bed and certain escape. 'You can't mean it.'

'Look at me,' he urged, and the pressure on her shoulder brought her slowly but surely around to face him. His features looked tight and controlled, while the fire in his golden eyes flared bright and bold, molten metal, hot and filled with desire.

*Desire for her.*

'Do I have to remove this towel to show you just how much I want to make love to you right now?'

Shock rendered her senseless. She shook her head, searching for the words she needed but lacking the vocabulary for situations like this. Because things like this just didn't happen to Morgan. Nobody had come near her since Evan, and not once in all the time they'd been together had they come close to anything as heated or sexual as what had just transpired here, in this bed.

*Oh, God, she was still in his bed.*

'I have to go,' she croaked, shrugging off his hand and scampering to the edge of the bed, fearful that he might try to stop her again. But he didn't make a move to prevent her leaving. Instead he just reclined on the bed with one hand supporting his head, so that she couldn't miss the full visual of what she'd just turned down.

In a flurry of frustration and rampant hormones she made a grab for her shoes and stood there with them in one hand, not bothering to put them on. 'This is crazy. We only met yesterday. We don't know the first thing about each other.'

'On the contrary,' he said, easing himself up from the bed like a jungle cat to stand before her, lean and long-limbed and golden-skinned.

It was his size that had her on the back foot straight away. Lying down, he'd looked masculine and supreme, the perfect facsimile of a god. Standing before her, he was a god, tall and broad-shouldered, and so terrifyingly large she felt insignificant in front of him.

He reached out and touched a hand to her hair. 'I know how much more beautiful you look with your hair down and wild around your face.' He shifted that same hand to run his knuckles down her cheek. 'And I know your skin feels soft as silk. And *you* know...'

She gazed up at him, trembling with a sudden burst of tenderness. She could fight his kisses—she could, she told herself. But this almost too gentle touch threatened her on another level.

She swallowed as his hand took one of her own. 'What do I know?'

'You know,' he said, as he took that hand and placed it flat over his chest, so that she could feel the strong, steady double beat under her palm, 'that every time my heart beats it is one less beat to the hour when we will make love. And until then you know I will be counting down.'

# CHAPTER FIVE

MORGAN gasped and wrenched her hand away, making a desperate lunge past him for the cabin door on legs that were far too unreliable right now for the task.

'Do you really want to go out looking like that? Do you want people to think you have already succumbed to my charms?'

She looked down at herself and a new wave of despair hit her. He was right. She was a mess—her skirt creased and twisted, her shirt hanging out and unbuttoned at the neck, her hair tumbling loose around her face. And while all she wanted to do was escape, on board Sheikh Tajik's own plane that hardly seemed a wise choice right now.

'Use the *en suite* here,' he offered, pulling open a door to a compartment built cleverly into the wall. 'You have nothing to fear, I assure you. I'll get dressed and be gone before you get out.'

She took a deep breath to steel herself. Why should she believe him? Though what choice did she have? She steered a course past him into the bathroom, trying to ignore once again the warmth that emanated from that almost naked body.

'You'd better lock the door,' he warned her, 'just in case

I decide that hour is now.' His words came accompanied with the hint of a wolfish smile that made her shut the door with unnecessary force and snib the lock as loud and defiantly as she possibly could. Damn the man! She wasn't about to take his advice on anything, but she'd been intending to use whatever locks the door had, regardless of his mocking tone.

Especially after that crack about counting down the heartbeats until they made love. What was that about? What right had he to say they would be making love *any* time?

*And why the hell did it excite her so much to think that they might?*

She leaned her head against the locked door and closed her eyes. What was happening to her?

In the space of twenty-four hours she'd gone from being in control, from knowing who she was and what she wanted, to nothing more than a confused mass of nerve-endings she'd never known existed. And Sheikh Tajik was the cause. He'd turned her inside out with his words and his body and the way that he wanted her. He'd turned her in a heartbeat from someone who had never considered jumping into bed with a man she barely knew to someone who had never been more sorely tempted and had had to fight with every scrap of resolve she had not to give in to temptation.

And she had been tempted. All that glorious flesh, the muscled back, the skin that had felt like satin under her hands. And those kisses that had drugged her senseless...

She sucked in air and pushed herself away from the door. She wouldn't let herself think about those kisses—so different from what she recalled of Evan's dispassionate affections. Little wonder when there was nothing dispassionate about Taj. He was passionate, intense, intent.

*Intent on taking her as his lover.*

The thought came with a tingling rush that pooled heavy and aching between her thighs as she took in for the first time her surroundings—the massive shower stall that filled the wall alongside her, and the beautiful timber and brass vanity unit standing opposite. Taj was all man—a real man—and he wanted her. And, while the concept was terrifying, at the same time it was electrifying.

What would it be like to make love with him? All that strength and power and passion? He would have to be an excellent lover, just by the way he'd made her feel—so alive and feminine and even sexy. And he'd been so tender—hadn't he'd comforted her when her nightmare had been at its worst, and so real, so dreadful?

Yes, they'd only just met, but was it wrong to be attracted to him? Was it wrong to wonder what it would be like to make love with him? And was it wrong for her body to want to?

Morgan raked one hand through her hair, frustrated that her thoughts were taking her into uncharted territory when what she needed right now was to get a grip on herself and her emotions if she was going to be able to go out there and pretend it was business as usual. The first step was to make herself at least look decent.

She flicked a switch on the vanity and an entire bank of lights above flashed into brilliance, illuminating the central mirror and making the room look more like some film star's make-up room than a mere bathroom. Though nothing, she reminded herself, was a mere anything on this plane.

Except for her.

She stepped closer to the mirror and let the full glare of the electric light bulbs rain down on her, revealing the full horror of her predicament.

It was worse than she'd thought. She touched a finger to her lips, plumped and pink, while her eyes looked back at her with a strange mix of wonder and fear. With her hair in disarray and her shirt askew it looked as if she'd been comprehensively tumbled already.

And under the scrutiny of the bright lights she asked herself what she was really doing here. She was a nobody. Hired to be Nobilah's companion. And yet all of sudden someone had changed the rules while she wasn't looking.

Suddenly she was a plaything to a sheikh—a sheikh obviously still mourning the loss of his fiancée and needing to slake his desires elsewhere. And no matter that she was attracted to him, no matter her body's response, no matter the smooth words he uttered with such apparent ease, she could never be more than that.

She'd promised herself after Evan that she'd never let herself be used again. Why would she let Taj do precisely that? The answer was patently simple.

*She wouldn't.*

Tajik liked that she wasn't easy. He pulled a clean shirt from the wardrobe tucked into the panelling and shrugged it over his shoulders. She'd been torn, he could tell, and he would have had her if he'd pressed, but it was more entertaining this way. Winning things, he'd found, was always more rewarding than taking them.

Besides, he'd always enjoyed a challenge, and Ms Fielding was proving to be a delightful challenge—and a delightful enigma. She was at the same time responsive in his arms and yet surprisingly coy. Perhaps Kamil had been too hasty in his assessment of Australian women? This one at least was doing her best to play hard to get, scampering from his bed as if the hounds of hell were after her.

He allowed himself a smile as he tucked the shirt into his trousers. Hound singular, he amended, giving his hair a flick through with his fingers, and, yes, he *was* after her.

Little did she know she didn't have much more time to run.

The heat took her by surprise as she stepped from the plane. A wall of heat that felt like a blast furnace. Morgan had always assumed she'd be able to cope with any temperatures the weather could throw at her after living in Australia all her life, but this heat ratcheted up the thermometer to extreme levels. Already her legs were suffocating under her stockings, her lungs were scorched with the hot air and her lips felt parched, every bit of moisture being lost to the desert-dry air.

And it wasn't desert-dry by accident, she mused, as she followed Nobilah down the stairs under a brilliant blue sky that went on for ever. For, while the airport looked like any other, with hangars and terminals edging the tarmac, and a clutch of planes and helicopters all bearing the El Jamal insignia, beyond the fences lay golden sands that stretched into the distance in all directions, with just the occasional stunted bush or palm somehow clinging to life to break the view.

And yet, despite the biting heat, the landscape held a wild beauty, untamed and magnificent, that resonated with her Australian roots. Whatever problems she faced with Taj, her enthusiasm for discovering more about this exciting country bubbled up inside her.

A robed chauffeur ushered them into a waiting limousine at the bottom of the steps, and she stepped into the air-conditioned interior with a sigh of relief at the contrast.

Nobilah smiled. 'Now you will understand why some of our people choose to escape Jamalbad in the hottest months of the year.'

Morgan could only empathise. Any hotter than this and it would be impossible to survive in such a land, surely. Then the door opened and Taj climbed into the vehicle, sending the temperature soaring even inside the car.

It was the first she'd seen of him since he'd left her locked in the *en suite* bathroom. Two hours it had taken her to rationalize his actions as nothing more than those of a bored traveller finding a ready companion in his bed. Two hours to convince herself that once back in his country he would hardly be concerned with the likes of her.

Two hours of effort that was now wiped away with one loaded look from those golden eyes. And one touch of his hand to his heart. So brief that anyone else would have missed the significance, to Morgan it was like a full-page ad. He hadn't been joking. He was counting down. His game, whatever game he was playing, wasn't over yet.

Briefly he greeted his mother, exchanging details of the flight, before turning back to Morgan.

'And what about you, Ms Fielding?' he asked, reclining into his seat as the car pulled smoothly away across the tarmac. 'Did the flight provide you with any memorable moments?'

She could feel her colour rising, she'd but be damned if she was going to give him the satisfaction of admitting she was rattled by his presence. 'Yes, in fact it did. Nobilah and I watched a good movie, and then she was kind enough to introduce me to some of your family members, courtesy of the portraits in the dining room.'

He raised his eyebrows. 'I can see how that would be the high point of any journey.'

'If there was anything else,' she told him innocently, 'it's nothing that comes to mind.'

His eyes narrowed, his mouth turned up in a half-smile, and she had the sinking feeling that instead of making it plain that she wasn't about to revisit what had happened in his stateroom she'd just issued him with the biggest challenge in the world. Yet what exactly had he been expecting her to say after what had happened—especially in front of his mother?

Besides, in the end nothing *had* happened. Not really. He'd been there when she'd come out of her nightmare, and he'd more or less taken advantage of the fact she'd been in his bed. In all truth, she hadn't made an effort to stop him until things had got way too intense. And she'd been a fool to let him kiss her again.

It was hardly the stuff fond memories were made of, and the only reason she couldn't get it out of her mind now was because she was determined she wasn't going to let it happen again—no matter what the Sheikh decreed.

To prove her resolve she turned her attention out of the tinted windows as Nobilah provided a running commentary. Now, *this* was memorable. Outside the airport twin rows of palms lined the road, and already the desert was making way for the odd low dwelling, and small communities that Nobilah named in turn.

'How far is it into Jamalbad City?' Morgan asked, only to be rewarded with a none too distant view of a cluster of office towers as they crested a small rise.

She pressed her face to the window, feeling more like an excited schoolgirl than a woman of twenty-five. Behind the flash of modern glass and steel towers stretching into the sky lay a backdrop of sparkling blue sea. It was like a mirage in the distance, a promise of paradise.

'And there is the palace,' said Nobilah, pointing out a building edging the sea. 'You can just see it from here.'

All she could see was an ornate domed central roof that gleamed in the sun, and layer upon layer of decorated arched windows. She realised it must be massive to appear so large from here.

'We'll be there in less than ten minutes,' Nobilah added.

They made it in five, passing colourful markets, or soukhs, on the way. Sheltered by awnings and favoured by a slight breeze from the sea, it was cooler here, and Morgan lowered her window and drank in the sights and sounds and heady scents. Women were dressed brightly, some in the more traditional garb that she'd expected, others wearing their own blend of western and Arab dress, whereas the men seemed to favour long white robes that flowed like water as they walked.

'It's exactly like you told me,' she said to Nobilah, unable to keep the excitement from her voice. This was the experience she had come for—to discover the Jamalbad of the older woman's stories, to see for herself the colours and culture of a different world. 'It's wonderful.'

'I am glad you approve of my country,' Taj said, as the car slid through a pair of richly decorated gates and onto a driveway circling a sprawling courtyard. 'It will make your stay much more enjoyable for everyone.'

She looked at him, trying to read his features, wondering whether there was some hidden meaning to his words.

His face and his eyes betrayed nothing but the certain knowledge that his fascination with her was not over yet.

And as he held her gaze something jolted inside her, causing her breath to catch and her heart-rate to kick up. She could no longer deny it. This excitement she was feeling right now couldn't simply be attributed to being in Jamalbad.

The truth was that she was falling for a man with fire-flecked eyes and golden skin. The truth was that, despite all her misgivings and uncertainties and fears, she knew in her heart that she was going to let him make love with her.

The truth was that she could hardly wait.

'Ms Fielding,' he said, holding out his hand to her as the chauffer swung the door open and Nobilah climbed out, 'your palace awaits.'

She blinked. She hadn't even realised they'd stopped. In a daze, she slid her own hand into his, feeling the connection spark like electricity between them. She looked into his eyes, witnessed something flare and flicker across their caramel depths, and knew that he'd felt it too.

And that strengthened her resolve. Whatever she was feeling, she knew he wasn't just talking words. She knew the connection was there. Whatever it was—attraction, desire, lust—they were on the same wavelength. He wasn't just using her because she was available. He wanted her just the same as she wanted him.

And he would make this trip truly memorable—of that she had no doubt.

Morgan let him guide her from the car out into the pillared portico that protected them from the sun's heat, her hand enclosed in his warm one. She refused to think about anything other than the coming night and what secret pleasures it might bring, which left her totally unprepared for the magnificence of the palace that stood before her.

From a distance it had looked massive, but close up she could fully appreciate the sheer scale of the complex. Instead of just one building, as she'd been expecting, lower buildings sprawled either side of the main palace, spreading out like the wings of a large bird.

But there was no time to dwell on the architecture—not when she came face to face with the welcome party awaiting them.

She recognised the man immediately from the portraits, though she didn't recognise the young woman standing alongside. She was beautiful, her eyes large, smoky and long-lashed, her caramel-coloured skin, clear and glowing. Qasim scowled down at Morgan and Taj disdainfully from under his headdress, the frown deepening momentarily when he caught sight of their locked hands. Self-consciousness made Morgan try to ease out of his grip, but if Taj noticed it he made no concession by letting her go.

'Excellencies.' Qasim bowed slightly and turned what might pass as a smile on his cousin and his mother, before greeting them in their own language. 'How delightful to see you back so early,' he added in English, presumably for Morgan's benefit. 'And who, may I ask, is this?' He turned his razor-sharp eyes on Morgan. 'Is this the woman hired to replace Fatima?'

'Your sources prove correct, my cousin. This is Murjanah Fielding.'

Qasim made no effort to greet her, or to welcome her to the country. 'Then I will ensure a room is made ready in the women's quarters. Abir,' he said, with a toss of his head towards the girl standing alongside, 'can show her the way.'

It sounded to Morgan like a dismissal, but when she made a move to comply and follow the girl, Taj tugged her back.

'That will not be necessary, Qasim. The woman is with me.'

Morgan reeled in shock at the blatant implication. But it was nothing to the expression she caught on Qasim's face.

'Excellency,' he blurted, obviously battling to regain his composure, 'I do not understand. You said this woman was employed as Nobilah's companion.'

'No, cousin. You said that. I merely agreed that that had been the basis on which she had been employed.'

'But now you are saying…'

'Now I am saying that I am presenting my intended sheikha and Jamalbad's next queen.'

# CHAPTER SIX

'What the hell was that all about?'

The thunderclap of the announcement had been made, stunned looks exchanged and the congratulations of Nobilah received—she'd seemed to be the only one thrilled with the news. Before Qasim had let fly with a torrent of protests. Not that Morgan had understood a word, but she'd been in no doubt of their meaning, and had been in complete agreement. Before she'd had a chance to offer her own protest, Taj had silenced them all with one harsh word and bustled her bodily deep into the palace and into a large private chamber.

Now she rubbed her wrist, where he'd clung to her, forcing her to go with him until he'd entered this room and spun her free. In the same action he'd thrown closed the door. The wonders of its decorations—the gold walls and brightly painted vaulted ceiling, the murals adorning each end of the room—earned no more than a glance.

'Well?' she demanded. 'I don't think it's too much to ask what the hell is going on. You told me I was coming here as Nobilah's companion.'

'Not at all. If you think back to our talk by the pool, I merely told you that you were needed in Jamalbad. You connected the dots in such a reckless fashion yourself.'

'Don't twist things so you can make out you're the innocent party here! *You* got me to Jamalbad, nobody else. What kind of game do you think you're playing?'

He took a step closer and she fought the instinctive urge to shrink away from him, instead standing firm, fighting for her ground.

His eyes had turned to agate, cold and uncaring. 'I assure you this is no game.'

'Then what was that garbage about me being your future wife? You were talking about me. *Me!* You have no right to suggest such a thi—'

'I have every right!'

This time she did take a step back, blown away by the vehemence of his reply. Still, she turned away, crossing her arms over her chest, shaking her head.

'Murjanah.' The red-hot anger from his voice had dissipated, but not the determination. In fact his words sounded horrendously clipped and impersonal. 'You are in my kingdom. I decide what happens here.'

She shivered at his ice-cold tone. 'You must be crazy! You don't make decisions for me. I'm leaving this nightmare right now.'

Morgan made a dash for the door, but he stopped her flight dead with one sure hand to her arm.

'Where do you think you are going?'

'To the airport. To get the first flight out of here home. *Anywhere*.'

'You think you can call up your Qantas here?'

'It's an airport, isn't it?' she retorted. 'There must be flights.'

'And they are *all* El Jamal aircraft.'

She kicked up her chin defiantly. 'Then I will fly El Jamal.'

'I own every plane in that fleet. You are not going anywhere. No one will touch you.'

'I will take a boat.'

Tajik shook his head, and she knew that he was going to claim the port as being under his control even before he confirmed it.

'Then I will swim!'

He sighed. 'Don't you think it is time to stop being so melodramatic?'

'How do you expect me to behave? I can't stay here. Not while you entertain these crazy dreams about me becoming your wife. It won't happen. I won't marry you! I'd rather become the bride of Frankenstein.'

This time he dared to laugh, the sound echoing around the vaulted ceiling, a rich, deep sound that tore her apart. Her open palm slammed against his cheek with a resounding crack.

A slash of colour turned his skin to dark caramel and the fires in his eyes flared into life under those heavy arched brows, giving his face a demonic look.

'That was unnecessary,' he hissed, his grip drawing her tighter in towards him.

'Not from my point of view,' she answered back, with a boldness that was becoming all too familiar to her around this man, although her frantic heartbeat betrayed her inner fears. Be damned if she was going to apologise, but if this was a man prepared to steal her away from her country and announce out of the blue that she was to become his queen what powers over her life and death did he *really* hold? Although one thing was certain. At least death would save her the indignity of becoming his wife!

'Ah, but you don't understand, my little pearl,' he told her, turning on the seductive quality in his voice that wrapped around her like satin ribbon and tugged on her senses. His hands trapped her wrists and pulled her arms down full length, so that she had no choice but to stand scant inches away from him. Through her clothes she could feel the heat emanating from him, the passion so tightly reined in under control as he battled to be reasonable. 'There need not be any marriage ceremony.'

She looked up at him, more confused than ever. 'There doesn't? Then I don't really have to marry you?'

'Of course not.' He smiled down at her benevolently, and for a moment she felt the first sweet taste of relief. 'Because, you see,' he continued, 'my simply decreeing that you will be my bride makes our marriage formal. Kamil has already taken care of the paperwork—what little there is to be filed. It is a wonderfully simple system here in Jamalbad, don't you agree?'

Sweetness turned instantly bitter. 'What? You decide who you're going to marry without a shred of agreement from your spouse to-be?' Fruitlessly she struggled against the manacle-like grip of his hands. 'What kind of prehistoric country is this, exactly?'

He gave a sharp tug on her wrists, reeling her in tighter, closer to his long, lean heat—heat that she didn't want to feel next to hers, heat that she didn't want to acknowledge, despite the effect it had on her own body as she was forced to stand so close to his.

'Do not insult my country,' he warned her in a tone that brooked no disagreement. 'We may do some things differently, but our culture is not to be so easily disregarded.'

'But you can't make decisions like this without consulting people!'

'And of course you are right. No betrothal can be sanctioned without the approval of the bride's parents.'

'My parents are both dead! How could anyone ask them?'

'An unfortunate truth which has served to provide some convenience in this matter. I have taken responsibility for you. I assure you, it has all been approved.'

Fury sparked from every cell in her body as she battled against his tight grip on her wrists. 'Not by me, it hasn't! *I* take responsibility for *me*!'

'It is done. There is no point fighting it.'

'I don't accept that. There must be someone else who would be mad enough to marry you. Or is that why you had to steal someone from so far away? Because all the women in Jamalbad had already turned you down flat?'

Tajik jerked her towards him, his jawline set rigid, his neck corded and straining tight. Too late she remembered his fiancée, killed in the same crash that had deprived him of his father. All too clearly she saw the pain slice across his eyes, sharp and jagged and real, and she swallowed, instantly regretting her words. But, damn him, why should she treat him with kid gloves when he was behaving like the ultimate Neanderthal?

'I could have chosen anyone for my bride,' he uttered low, so threateningly close to her face that his heated breath fanned her cheek. 'But of all women, with just one look, I chose you!'

'Then unchoose me! I will not be used. I won't let you.'

'Who said anything about being used? This arrangement is of convenience to us both. It is time I took a wife. You are clearly in need of a husband. This marriage will suit us both, if you let it.'

Morgan laughed crazily. 'In need of a husband? Says who?'

'Says the fact you have no boyfriend or lover. Says the way you dress—like you encase yourself in armour. How were you ever to find yourself a husband with such steel cladding around you?'

'But I've had boyfriends!' she protested, the uncanny accuracy of his barbs spearing her to the core. 'At one stage I was even engaged to be married.' She glossed over the minor technicality that her fiancé had been gay, knowing it would hardly further her cause. 'I'm not some charity case that needs rescuing. And I'm not grateful that you are so intent on saving me from my spinsterhood. Where I come from people marry for love. I don't imagine you have any understanding of the concept.'

He released her so suddenly she swayed on her feet. Her hands rubbed the places where he'd held her as he strode purposefully away. And then he turned. 'I don't expect you to love me.' His voice was flat and lifeless, his eyes clouded and she knew he meant every word—and, even more, those words that he'd left unspoken hung in the air like a promise. *Just as I will never love you.*

*Which suited her just fine.*

'Just as well. You're the last man on earth I could ever love. In fact, I *hate* you.'

He surveyed her, his brow arching, his features gentling. 'Come,' he said softly, as if he were settling a recalcitrant child, 'I know this has been difficult for you. But there is no need for histrionics.'

She shook her head even as he came closer, lifting both hands to her shoulders. She flinched away but he continued, sliding his fingers around to cup her neck, his thumbs stroking her skin at the nape. His eyes gazed down at her, the clouds gone, the coals contained therein alive once more with heat.

'I think you're confused. You don't really hate me. What you meant to say is that you *want* me.'

'You're out of your mind. You have no right—'

'So we are back to this.' He sighed theatrically, as if her protests were a mere formality. 'When are you going to accept that I have *every* right, given this is my country? The sooner you get used to it, the better for everyone concerned. You are mine now.'

Shock all but punched the battle from her body. She was *his*? This was the twenty-first century, and she was an Australian citizen. This could not be happening to her.

'You can't *own* people. You don't own me. You never will!'

His eyes glinted dangerously, his lips curving into a wicked smile. 'Is that a challenge you are making? I do so enjoy a challenge…'

She turned her head away, recognizing the sheer futility of trying to reason with this man. It was like arguing with a brick wall.

'Understand me,' he said, tilting her chin back towards him. 'What I want here in Jamalbad. I get. And I want you, my little pearl. Just as I will have you.'

'And what about what I want?' she whispered.

He looked down at her with such a look of pity that she wanted to turn her face away again, but he held it firm. And then he smiled—a predator's smile, the smile of a man who was used to taking what he wanted when he wanted, regardless of the consequences. 'I will be all you want and more.'

Anger turned incendiary at his arrogance—or was that just the primitive thrill that exploded through her at his words, terrifying her with its implications and threatening to undo her completely? She tried to push him away, her strength returning in a sudden rush because she knew that one way or another she had to get away from him. But he only snared her wrists in his hands once again.

'Let go of me,' she protested.

'Why? So you can hit me again? I think not.'

'You have to let go of them some time.'

'When I let them go, I expect your hands to be doing something entirely more satisfying.'

She sneered. 'Not likely. When you let go of them they'll be clawing your eyes out!'

'And I was hoping they would be clawing my back in ecstasy.'

'Fat chance!'

'You wound my manly pride. Does that not concern you?'

'Doesn't it concern *you* that you are detaining a woman who does not want to be detained? A woman who does not want to be claimed as your own? I want to go home. And I want to go home now!'

He let go her wrists so suddenly that she had no time to react before he wrapped her in his arms and hauled her in close. 'Did anyone ever tell you that you talk too much?' he muttered, his face descending closer to hers. 'It is definitely time someone shut you up.'

Morgan gasped, bewildered, his change in tactics leaving her totally unprepared for the onslaught that was to come as she slammed against his body full force. The certain knowledge that he was fully aroused gave her one crystal-clear moment of panic before the certain knowledge that he was about to kiss her gave that panic wings.

'No!' she protested, as much for her own benefit as for his.

She yanked her head to the side before his lips met their mark, but it proved pointless as his mouth meshed instead with her throat. A groan came unbidden as his lips and tongue lashed her skin, suckling, cajoling, laving. *Persuading*.

Fruitlessly she bucked and twisted in his arms. His grip was unrelenting, his mouth performing magic on her skin. She felt her breasts swell and peak under his ministrations and she cursed her body for its betrayal. Why did what he was doing seem more important than what he was depriving her of? How could her body so easily forget what she'd been fighting for?

And then came a cry of frustration that he could do this to her—reduce her to a mess of nerve-endings in so short a time. 'Damn you,' she whispered, even as her body hummed for more.

'You can damn me all you like,' he rasped, 'so long as this night you give me the honour of loving you.'

Her mind drank in his words as quickly as her body drank in his caresses. How could this be happening to her? He said he'd chosen her—but why her? Why Morgan Fielding, of all people? It made no sense. But no sense became perfect sense as he glided his hand along the curve of her hip to her waist, and then higher, so that in the end his hand cupped her breast. She gasped with the sudden heat of it, gasping into his mouth and involuntarily letting him know just how much his touch affected her.

'Please…' she murmured, not knowing exactly what she was pleading for—an end to his ministrations or a quickening of the pace. If he was going to take her, why couldn't he just do it. Why did he have to make it so damned pleasurable?

He squeezed her breast and her back arched against him instinctively, her spine and knees melting as her recently freed arms, now too languid to fight, reached for him, clinging to his shoulders lest she fall to the floor.

Besides, there was no point fighting, she told herself. Because he was going to take her anyway. Wasn't it better to let him have his way and let him think she was falling in with his plans? Then, later, she would enlist someone's help—not Nobilah, because for some reason she seemed taken with Taj's crazy idea, but maybe the young girl, Abir. She might help her escape…

And then he caressed her breast again, and she forgot how to think—knew only how to feel. He groaned as he massaged her sensitive flesh, his thumb rolling lazily over her exquisitely hard nipple, sending jagged bolts of lightning coursing down to her core. 'By Allah, you are magnificent,' he told her. 'I knew from the very beginning that you would be so. It will be my honour to pleasure you. But first let us be rid of these accursed clothes that bind you tighter than a drum.'

One singular moment of panic registered—another zip of excitement blotted it out as his mouth pursued hers, trapping it and subjecting it to his expertise. His fingers found her buttons, manoeuvring two clear of their button-holes before impatience got the better of him and she felt her shirt pulled apart, the buttons ripped clean away.

'Taj!' she cried out, trying ineffectually to cover herself.

'Your clothes are ridiculous for this climate,' he growled, dispensing with her efforts and sweeping the rent fabric from her shoulders along with her bra straps, unclipping it behind her in the same deft movement. She felt the sweep of air as her upper body and breasts became exposed both to the air and to his view, but it was his groan of adoration that reigned supreme in her psyche.

'Magnificent,' he purred, as seductively as a jungle cat, his golden eyes glowing like flame. 'So perfect.' And he dipped his head and took one peaked bud between his teeth. This time her knees did buckle with the sheer erotic pleasure of his mouth.

He gathered her up in his arms, her weight no burden, and returned his attention to her mouth. Somewhere along the line her clip had fallen free, and now his hand wove its way through her hair, directing her mouth to the exact angle he needed to plunder its depths. She clung to him, beyond caring where he was taking her, beyond caring about anything other than that soon he would be making love to her. Soon she would feel the power of this man inside her. And right now nothing else mattered.

Later, she told herself. Later she would find a way to escape.

Tajik carried her deeper into the suite, lowering her at his destination. 'I have waited for this moment ever since we met,' he said, and his words worked a kind of magic she did not understand beyond the simple pleasure of being wanted, a woman desired by a man. With it came an insane satisfaction that she hadn't wasted herself on Evan, who hadn't wanted a woman at all. Whatever his faults, whatever insane ideas he held about her future, Tajik would be a man in bed. She had no doubt of that. He knelt beside her, looking down at her, his eyes molten with want, and a new fear took hold—would she be woman enough for him?

Then he pulled apart his shirt with the same reckless-ness that had finished hers, scattering buttons in every di-rection, and she didn't know if it was his determination to have her, the sight of that golden chest or both that sheer took her breath away.

His shoes and trousers were all but wrenched off, and once again she was faced with the gleaming perfection that was Taj. Only this time it was black silk and not a towel that separated her from that part of him that she craved the most.

And then even that scrap was gone, and her fears returned tenfold. He was so like the famous palace his name reminded her of—unique, sculpted, magnificent. A stallion of a man. And even while she could feel the moisture building between her aching thighs, secretly she feared she would never be able to accommodate him.

He let her gaze drink him in, pausing as if on the cusp of something significant, before he leant down and cupped her breasts, his touch so soft, so gentle, that she wanted to cry out in desperation. His hands slowly tracked down her sides, his fingers delving below the waistband of her skirt.

He growled in frustration. *'This,'* he hissed through his teeth as he forced his hands behind her. *'Off,'* he asserted as his fingers found her zip, dragging it down. *'Now!'*

With both hands he yanked the skirt free of her hips and legs and flung it carelessly away.

'Yes,' he muttered, as if to himself, as he gazed upon her. 'And these.' She found her underwear and stockings similarly dispensed with, and it was his turn to gaze upon her.

'I have waited for this from the moment we met,' he said, his face a mask of control, his breathing as tight and short as her own. 'And now I will have you.'

He inserted one knee between hers, dropping down on one arm to kiss her again and trace the feminine curve of her cheek, the labyrinth of her ear. And even as he continued to make love to her with his mouth his hand swept down the curve of her throat, the rise of her breast. He lingered there momentarily, increasing her pleasure, increasing her need, before his large hand moved on, scooping over the flesh of her stomach and over the jutted curve of her hip. She almost cried out when his fingers dipped lower, parting her curls, delving into her most feminine place.

Her legs seemed to part of their own accord, and his other knee moved in to join the first. His skilful fingers circled that screaming tight bud, causing her hips to squirm and her back to arch, driving her head deeper into the pillows with the exquisite torture. And then it was a new sensation she felt—his fingers testing her at her very epicentre.

'So slick, my perfect one,' he murmured against her skin, as she felt the strange and wonderful sensation of his finger sliding inside her. And still it wasn't enough, still she wanted more, *needed more.*

'And so tight…'

He turned from torrid and almost frantic to rigid in an instant. His mouth withdrew, his hand was gone and his tight mask of control had disappeared, replaced by a frown that coupled bewilderment with damnation. And all at once she felt ashamed and exposed, foolish for being swept away on a tide of passion with a man she barely knew. With a man who could reduce her to this and then leave her high and dry, just as he had done with his kiss.

For too long, it seemed, he didn't utter a word, though it was probably only the time it took for him to take two raggedly drawn breaths. Then his words sliced through the air like an accusation.

'You are a virgin.'

He made it sound like some kind of affliction, adding to the disgust she already felt for herself. 'Is that a problem?' she retorted. 'I thought you had an issue with women who were too free with their favours. Or was this just another of your tricks to prove my suspect morals?'

He cursed and swung himself away from her, pacing across the room, a rampaging stallion refused his mare. He swung back. 'What are you talking about?'

Morgan bristled, gathering the coverlet around her. As if he didn't know! 'Haven't you been testing me ever since we met? That kiss last night, what happened on the plane—you told me you didn't want anyone who might sleep around, and yet you've done everything you could to test me.'

'Is that what you really believe? Maybe I wanted to kiss you. Maybe I wanted to make love to you all along.'

'And maybe this is fantasyland, where your every dream comes true!'

His face glowed with his anger. 'It was inevitable that we make love. You should have told me you are a virgin!'

'Maybe you should have thought to ask!'

'And would you have told me?'

'No bloody way!' She wrapped herself deeper in the coverlet, wanting to hide, wanting to run away, wanting to cry with the sheer injustice of it all.

Dammit, she would *not* cry!

Instead she pulled the cover more tightly around her, wrenching it from the bed as her bare feet hit the floor.

'Where do you think you are you going?'

His booming voice did nothing to calm her fractured nerves.

'I want my clothes,' she said. 'And then I'm getting out of here.'

'You cannot leave.'

She picked up her skirt. Found one stocking and gave up on the rest of her underwear. She sniffed, her throat close to cracking. 'I'll find a way.'

'You are going nowhere!' His hand latched onto her arm, wheeling her around.

'I hate you!' she cried. 'Why can't you believe me? I *hate* you.' She turned her face away, but his fingers directed her chin back, one long finger reaching out to catch the fat tear rolling down her cheek.

'And are you mad at me,' he asked, his voice more gentle, 'because I have brought you here to be my wife?' His eyes looked searchingly into hers. 'Or because just now I didn't give you the release your body craves?'

She glared up at him, resenting the way he could read her so well and not wanting to delve too deeply into that question herself. 'Don't flatter yourself.'

Tajik uttered his chosen name for her on a sigh. 'I knew you were perfect. But in my wildest dreams I did not realize just how much. Don't you see? You are a virgin, and for that kind of treasure you should be prized, not pillaged.'

Morgan eyed him suspiciously, afraid to let his words massage her bruised soul. 'So what's that supposed to mean? Now you're planning on offering me up to the gods as some virgin sacrifice? I promise you, it would be preferable to anything else you have in store.'

He laughed, the rich strong sound filling the room and further feeding her ire. She swung round, determined to get away, but he snagged her easily in her makeshift robe and bundled her into his arms for the journey back to the bed. He sat down, keeping her in his lap like a small child who needed comforting.

'And what exactly do you think the gods would favour me with for such a fine sacrifice?'

'I don't know,' she stammered, refusing to look at him, her body trembling in the wake of all that had transpired between them—for all that that had *almost* transpired between them—but beyond caring whether she further offended him. 'Maybe you could ask for a personality transplant.'

His reaction surprised her. He laughed, and kissed the top of her head. 'You are so different to how I imagined you would be when we first met. You have a spirit I didn't see.'

She couldn't argue with that. She seemed to have developed a spirit she'd never known before either. 'Maybe that's because I've not had much experience in getting whisked away by sheikhs.'

His hand found her chin, giving her no choice but to face him. Still she kept her eyes down, avoiding his golden gaze. 'Look at me,' he said, his voice a gentle instruction.

She wavered, but she knew that eventually she would have to comply. Would be compelled to comply. She lifted her gaze till it collided with his powerful golden one.

'You are a woman among women,' he told her. 'Your gift is too precious to take like a rutting bull. Tomorrow at my desert palace will be a feast in honour of our marriage, followed by two weeks of celebrations. All the tribal chiefs will be in attendance. There I will present you to them as my wife.'

She waited while he spoke. Waited until after he had finished speaking for him to continue and tell her more. But he was silent, and it was with a shaky voice that she was forced to ask the question.

'That's it? That's all that happens?'

His arms cradled her warmly as he shook his head, the fires in his eyes rekindling with heat. 'No, that's not all. Because after the feasting, after the fires have died down and the entire galaxy is alight in the night sky, only then will I make love to you in the way you so properly deserve.'

## CHAPTER SEVEN

A CONVENIENT virgin. When he'd told Kamil he would find someone who would pass for a convenient virgin, he'd had no idea just how convenient Murjanah would be.

*Or how much a virgin.*

Tajik lay back on his bed, his hands behind his head. She was a find, a rare pearl indeed. He'd figured her as inexperienced—but to be untouched? She had told him she'd been engaged to be married. How could any man have neglected a fiancée so clearly responsive? It was his loss, whoever the fool was. Right now she must be tossing and turning in anticipation of the completion tomorrow night would bring. It would be his pleasure to introduce her to the delights of the bedroom. Her remaining resistance would crumble like an eggshell and she would be his.

*His and no one else's.*

A feeling akin to pride filled his chest. Until now he hadn't cared if she'd had one or two other lovers. To him it had not been an issue when he had merely been looking for an easy fix to the problem of Qasim.

And yet now that concept appealed more and more.

Why should that be? He looked to one side, his eyes seeking out the photograph next to his bed of the woman with the wide dark eyes and enigmatic smile. If she had lived he would be married to her now, and none of this would be necessary.

Beautiful Joharah, with her meek manner and accommodating nature. Joharah would never have argued with him like this woman did. She would never have been bold enough to tell him that he was crazy and mad. She would never have dared hint that *any* woman in Jamalbad would turn him down, let alone every single one of them.

He allowed himself a smile at the memories, eventually letting his gaze slide back to the ceiling. His convenient virgin was proving more entertaining than he'd ever imagined.

She would escape. Nothing had changed that fact. Not even the words that had threatened to seduce her with precision-like accuracy—words that she could not get out of her head. "I will make love to you in the way you so properly deserve." Every single time she played them over in her mind it sent shivers of anticipation through her.

He'd been so gentle with her after telling her that. He'd tucked her into bed and gently kissed her on the forehead, telling her he would have something sent up for her and that then she should sleep, but that if she needed anything he was as close as the adjoining bed chamber.

He'd been so gentle and caring and concerned...

But that changed nothing. She'd been brought here for reasons other than those she'd been led to believe. She was being refused her freedom and a passage home. He had no right to treat her this way—no right at all. No matter how damned omnipotent he claimed to be. The first chance she had, she would find the means to escape.

Only now…

Dressed in one of the robes he'd provided as her lavish new wardrobe, she looked out of the passenger window of the vehicle she shared with Nobilah as the fleet of four-wheel drives sped along the sandy terrain, eating up the dunes as the party surged deeper and deeper into the desert.

For once the harsh beauty of the landscape eluded her, lost as she was in the dreadful truth of her predicament. From the city she might have a chance, disguised and hidden amongst the teeming market crowds. She might have a fighting chance. But how was she going to escape from here? Where would she run? How would she ever find her way home?

Beside her Nobilah talked excitedly about the wedding plans, and what would happen and who they would meet. She mentioned some names, a Sheikh Khaled and his queen Zafira, and she tried to focus and share some of the older woman's excitement for the occasion. But it was impossible. The endless climb and descent over the dunes had her stomach lurching, and after a while all the names blurred into just one more insurmountable hurdle she had to face.

How could she carry this off? How could she be expected to perform as queen of anywhere? She didn't belong here. She knew nothing that would prepare her for the role Taj seemed so determined for her to fill.

For a while she drifted, thinking about her sister and the baby, wondering how long it would be before she saw them again. If ever. The thought stabbed her like a knife. This wasn't how she had seen her future panning out.

'How do you like your new robes? I think that amber shade is wonderful with your hair and eyes.'

Morgan looked down at the richly embroidered abaya she was wearing—one of more than a dozen Taj had had delivered to her room this morning. Despite her protests that she had her own clothes, he'd insisted, and for once she had to concede that maybe he was right. While she'd at first missed the security of her fitted suits, this fabric was as light as air, and slipped over her skin like silk, cool and wonderful in the heat. Such a change from her formal business attire, it had instantly made her feel more feminine, even a little sexy with the way it hinted at curves hidden below—curves she was for the first time coming to appreciate.

'It's beautiful,' she admitted. 'And surprisingly cool.'

'I'm so glad. It can be difficult when so much in your life is changing so suddenly. It is good that you are not finding things too much of a challenge.'

Morgan smiled and saw her chance. Nobilah was offering her the perfect opportunity to test out how sympathetic she might be to her plight. But she knew she would still have to approach the topic sensitively.

'Nobilah,' she ventured, 'about this whole wedding deal. I'm not entirely sure—'

The older woman patted her hand. 'Of course you are nervous. That is to be expected.'

'But I honestly thought I was coming to Jamalbad to be your companion.'

Nobilah squeezed her hand. 'Now you can be both my companion and my daughter-in-law. Who could ask for more? And I am so pleased my son has decided to move on and find himself a wife. I know what it is like to mourn, and he is too young to give himself up to that dark place. You are like a breath of fresh air for Jamalbad—a clear sign the bad times have passed and that our time for mourning is over.'

Morgan held out her hands in an impassioned plea, feeling frustrated with the woman's easy acceptance of her situation. 'But Taj and I have only just met. We hardly know each other.'

Nobilah only smiled and wrapped her two hands in her own, squeezing them gently. 'Then you will have an entire marriage to get to know one another. And, believe me, it will still not be long enough to appreciate all there is in your partner—' She broke off the conversation and turned away, a slight tremor in her voice giving away her lingering sadness.

Morgan turned her attention out of the window to the seemingly endless dunes, assuming the subject was closed and recognising that there was no point pressing her case with the older woman anyway.

'I met Ashraf for the first time on our wedding day.'

Morgan turned back in shock, and Nobilah gave a small chuckle at her reaction. 'Of course I had heard stories of how valiant he was, and how handsome and strong. And he had seen a picture of me and decided then and there I was to be his wife.'

'But you loved him. You must have—all those years you had together.'

The older woman gave a wistful smile. 'Yes, I loved him. Although it was probably more like awe on our wedding day that such a perfect specimen with royal blood would choose a girl from a lowly village. Our love grew every day, and grew.' She smiled. 'He was a good man, my husband.' She nodded, smiling to herself. 'Taj is very much like him.'

*Was* he a good man? Morgan wondered. How could he be described as good when he'd done as much as kidnap her? He could be ferocious, his anger swelling up and crashing down again like a tidal wave. And yet he could be so tender—the way he'd cradled her last night, as if he knew she needed comforting, and the way he'd held back from roughly taking her when he'd been clearly so ready and had had no need to wait.

Did those things make a good man? She wished she knew. Right now she'd never been more confused.

They settled into silence as the vehicle traversed dune after dune, each of them lost in their own thoughts, until they came across a herd of animals, their long horns pointing proudly into the sky. Fascinated by the noble-looking white antelope, with their bold black markings and their sweet fawns, Morgan asked what they were.

Nobilah looked across and smiled. 'We must be getting close. They are Arabian oryx. You will see many more around the palace. Some are quite tame.'

'They are not afraid of man?'

'They are protected here. Their numbers were in decline for many years. Tajik convinced his father that they should be protected, and this is now considered a reserve where they may run free.'

Taj had done that? Morgan filed that piece of information away. She hadn't picked him as an animal lover—not that they'd had any time to talk about anything beyond how high-handedly he was behaving.

Eventually the sand dunes gave way to more scrubby terrain, and there, on the horizon, she could see it. The desert palace. Surrounded by palms marking an oasis in this sunburnt land, the central building stood as if it had been carved from the sand itself, its walls glowing like gold in the afternoon sun. As they drew closer she could see an assembly of low buildings like homes set amongst the palms. Designed like Bedouin tents, Nobilah told her, their roofs provided a wide canopy of shade around each building.

'What are they for?' Morgan asked.

'They're suites designed to accommodate visiting dignitaries and visitors in privacy. Also there is Taj's own apartment, which you will soon see.'

Morgan frowned. 'Wouldn't it make sense security-wise to have his accommodation within the palace?'

'In troubled times, you're right, and there is a suite of rooms kept for him for just that purpose. But our land has been peaceful for some years now. With Tajik's leadership there is no reason that will not continue. And look,' she added brightly, pointing out of the window. 'Beyond you can see the tents of the tribal leaders' groups, who have all come for the celebration.'

Morgan couldn't help but stare in wonder, a feeling of excitement seeping into her veins. There must be dozens of circular tents staked into the ground, colourful banners and flags flying from each one and sending the clear message that this was indeed a time for celebration.

And it was equally clear that this couldn't have been organised just yesterday. Even with Kamil's organisational expertise, it would have been impossible to pull all this off within twenty-four hours. Which could only mean that her fate had been sealed earlier—maybe from the first moment they had met.

A flush of impossible excitement coursed through her. Nobilah kept telling her how much like his father Taj was. And Taj had told her he had decided at first sight that she was to be his sheikha.

He'd made it plain that this was not a love-match, but

could there be chance that this marriage of convenience would become something more real, given time, just as his own parents' marriage had? Could there be some chance that he might actually come to love her, in spite of his claims that she need never love him?

It was a romantic notion that seemed to have no place in either the modern world or her own predicament—especially when she should be thinking solely of escape. It was merely ego, she insisted, that made the concept that he'd chosen her, out of all the women in the world, somehow exciting. It was ego that made her wonder how hard it might be to make him love her.

Ego, or forbidden fantasy?

Did it matter? Either way, she could not deny that anticipation for what the evening would bring was building inexorably inside her—a pressure cooker of waiting, a slow simmering of tension that built as the hours progressed.

This coming evening he would finish what he had started last night. This coming evening he would take her. She squeezed her eyes shut as the memories of his touch played over and over in her mind—the same memories that brought a strange kind of terror to her heart and yet unfurled an aching need between her thighs. She shifted sideways in her seat, gazing unseeingly out of the window. How was it possible for a man, a virtual stranger, to make her respond so readily? To make her feel so much? How could it be possible for Morgan Fielding, professional virgin, to come so undone so quickly?

They arrived at the palace in grand style, but there was no time to admire the spacious rooms and tasteful decorations of carved oryx and colourful wall-hangings, as both

Nobilah and Morgan were whisked away to the women's quarters by a clutch of giggling women, their eyes beautifully made up, their bodies adorned with colourful robes and golden jewellery.

The next few hours passed in a blur of scented baths and fragrant oils, of massage and pampering like Morgan had never known.

And then, they told her, it was time. They styled her hair into lush glossy curls and dressed her in silken underwear, and then a slip so gossamer-thin as to be translucent. Over the top they wrapped a robe spun with golden thread, with hand stitched jewels in the panels at her neckline and wrists. It was a gown so beautiful it brought tears to her eyes as she stared at her reflection.

So this was what a desert queen looked like?

Another moment of panic took her. She knew not the first thing about these people, or this country. She could speak not a word of their language. How could she pretend to be their queen?

And yet nobody here seemed concerned. Instead the women all stood around, applauding their efforts and telling her in broken English how beautiful she was.

And she felt it. Somewhere in the past few days she had been transformed from an uptight PA with a chip on her shoulder and an aversion to men to a princess bride.

The women escorted Nobilah to the banquet hall first, to take her place alongside her son, before they returned for Morgan. They chattered as they led her from the women's quarters, the excitement in their voices unmistakable, while she felt numb, her senses so overburdened they had shut down.

What was she doing, going along with all this? This was

*marriage*, to a man in a country half a world away from her own, a marriage she had not even agreed to, and yet here she was, being led like the proverbial lamb to the slaughter.

From somewhere came the scent of meat on a spit and spices and herbs, and it was enough to almost turn her stomach. Oh, yes, it might well have been herself she smelt cooking.

Panic gripped her anew as the door to the large banquet hall was pulled open to admit them. Strains of music floated out to her, along with the general hubbub of celebratory conversation, and the noise fed into her stress. Was this what she wanted? Didn't she even have a say?

And then she saw him, sitting on cushions at the head of the room alongside Nobilah. He was dressed in traditional robes edged with gold, the first time she'd seen him wearing them, but she neither mistook his strong features and golden eyes nor missed the way those eyes widened in appreciation as they drank her in, the way the red coals flared up inside them. Using just his strong legs, he pushed himself to stand, and it was then that the robes showed off her husband to full advantage. He looked magnificent, the golden-edged robes adding to his aura of power and mystique.

As if responding to some silent order, the women around her peeled away and merged into the crowd until only she remained. The room within fell silent as he held out his hand to her, summoning her to enter the room and join him. When she hesitated she caught his prompt—a slight nod, an urge to action.

Still her feet rebelled. She could run now—turn and run back through the palace. But then where? She would be caught before she reached the doors, even if she knew which way lay the entrance. Or she could go through with this, knowing she had little other choice, and take her chance to escape some time later, when he thought that she was bent sufficiently to his will. Nobody at home would take this marriage seriously. It would be annulled in a heartbeat. It would be just as if it had never happened— just like waking up from a bad dream. All she had to do was go through with this now, and then let him make love to her later. Would that be such a hardship?

*Not if the way he'd made her feel last night was any indication.*

And so her feet moved, slowly and painstakingly taking her to the man with fire in his eyes and passion at his heart. A good man or a bad man? Did it really matter when she would not be staying any longer than the time it took to regain her freedom?

The room erupted into cheers and wild applause as she entered, but her eyes were not for the crowd spread out on cushions across the massive banquet hall. Tajik held her eyes and refused to let them go, drawing her across the carpet like a magnet.

He took her hand and she gasped as something sparked between them, causing the coals in his eyes to flare once more. One side of his mouth turned up. 'You are a goddess,' he told her. 'I have indeed been blessed.'

In spite of herself, his words warmed her heart. And she didn't want them to. He must not be kind to her, or gentle, or make her forget what he had done when he had imposed his will on hers.

But still she looked up at him, unable to prevent herself being drawn to the man before her. She knew she was in reality no goddess, but she had no doubt that there could be no closer facsimile of a god than this man standing before her, proud and magnificent and in his own special way beautiful.

Tajik waited until the crowd's cheers had died down to a general hubbub below the music before drawing her down onto the cushions where he sat between Nobilah and Qasim.

Nobilah welcomed her warmly with a kiss to each cheek. Beside Qasim sat the beautiful smoky-eyed girl who had been on the steps of the palace when she'd arrived in Jamalbad City. The girl peeked shyly at her through half lowered lashes, while Qasim merely nodded in her direction, the crooked smile he offered her unconvincing when coupled with the look of utter scorn in his eyes.

But right now she needed allies, and maybe the girl would be useful, so when she had a chance she held out a hand to her. 'Hello,' she said, hoping something of her message might be understood. 'We met briefly on the steps yesterday. It's nice to see you again.'

The girl blinked at her, her eyes wide and unsure, her lips slightly parted in surprise, before putting out a tentative hand of her own—only to have it thrust away by Qasim in between. He uttered something low and guttural in Taj's ear, only to have the man beside her stiffen before shooting back a heated volley of his own. Qasim's glare narrowed even more in response.

Morgan shuddered. 'What was all that about?' she asked, as Taj turned back towards her.

'Qasim was insisting on a medical examination to ensure you are a virgin.'

She looked at him, aghast. 'And what did you tell him?'

'I told him that would not be necessary. That I had already confirmed your innocence with an examination of my own.'

Colour rose in a tide, burning her cheeks and face, and she was so shocked she barely noticed that Qasim had risen from his cushions and disappeared, dragging the young girl with him.

'And your reaction,' Taj continued, taking her hand in his own, 'was all he needed to know my words are true.'

'And what if I hadn't been—a virgin?' She stumbled over the last two words, unfamiliar with talking about such issues with anyone, let alone a man she barely knew.

'In that case,' he said with a flick of his hand, as if it were inconsequential, 'I would have seen to it that your virginity was restored for one night.'

'You can do that, can you? Next you'll be claiming you can cure baldness and fix global warming.'

He chuckled, in spite of her snippy rejoinder, and held up one hand. 'I am the Sheikh. All things are possible.'

'How about letting me go?'

His features went from warm to granite-like hardness in a blink, the red coals in his eyes turning to ice chips.

'You are my wife now. That is not an option.'

'But you said—'

'I said that is not an option! Now, eat and drink something,' he said, filling a goblet with what looked like wine and passing it to her. 'You will need your strength and more for later on.'

The wedding feast seemed interminable, and it appeared to Morgan that she would need all her strength just to get through it, let alone what might come after. There were endless rounds of courses and sweetmeats, non-stop entertainment, and more people to meet, it seemed, than she had met in her entire life. A continual queue of guests lined up to greet her after the meal. She would never remember a fraction of the names.

Then came a familiar accent amongst the crowd of well-wishers as a woman in a stylish blue abaya burst through the crowd.

'Hey there, Aussie,' she said, a smile lighting up her beautiful features.

Morgan was so taken aback she could only stare, letting herself be wrapped in a heartfelt hug. 'When Khaled told me Sheikh Tajik had taken an Australian wife, I couldn't wait to meet you. It is going to be so good to have a friend close by!'

'I don't understand,' Morgan said, shaking her head, wondering why the name sounded familiar, half laughing as the woman let her go, only to grab hold of both her hands.

A tall, good-looking man stepped forward. 'Please forgive my wife. She is clearly too excited to introduce herself. I am Sheikh Khaled Al Ateeq, your neighbour across the border in Jebbai, and this,' he said, wrapping a possessive arm around his wife's waist, is my beautiful wife Sapphire—or Zafira, as we know her here.'

'You can call me Sapphy,' she said, still grinning wildly. 'It's so good to meet you. It's going to be fabulous having someone I can talk to.'

'Do you get lonely here?'

Sapphy laughed. 'Oh, no, never lonely. It'll just be great to be able to hear an Aussie accent every now and then.'

Morgan smiled back, the germ of an idea forming in the back of her mind. Sapphy was a stranger in this part of the world too. Surely she would understand her plight?

The line was moving on, Sapphy and her sheikh already passing by.

'I will see you again?' she asked, reaching out a hand to Sapphy.

The woman in blue turned back. 'Of course. We'll be here for the whole two weeks of celebration. I'll introduce you to our two-year-old terrors, Amid and Kahlil, whenever I can pin them down long enough.'

Morgan nodded, feeling better than she'd felt since she arrived in Jamalbad. There was hope, no matter what Taj decreed. There was an option after all…

She had no idea of the time, but at last the line dwindled, and other people, including Nobilah, drifted away. Those left settled into small family groups. Middle Eastern music played softly in the background—a beguiling, bewitching sound that stirred her senses.

She should have felt tired, she knew, and ordinarily she would have after the last few days she'd had, but it was impossible to feel anything but tense with the man half reclining on the cushions so close beside her.

If this part of the proceedings was winding down, it could only mean one thing—that the next part of the evening was drawing closer. A now familiar shiver of anticipation moved through her, keeping her senses on red alert. Oh, no, whatever the time, there was no way she was going to feel tired any time soon.

'Are you cold, my wife?' he asked, sitting up and wrapping a hand around her shoulders, his fingers stroking her arm through her robe, sending more involuntary tremors through her.

'Not really,' she answered, truthfully enough. Though

in no way was she prepared to admit that it was fear and trepidation for what lay ahead that was the root cause of her anxiety.

'Then what is it that makes you tremble? You're not tired?'

'No!' she said, much too quickly, bringing a smile to his lips.

'I am glad. It would not be good for you to sleep through your wedding night.'

Not much chance of that, she mused, as the music picked up in both tempo and volume. It had been impossible to sleep when the man didn't occupy her bed. How much more impossible was it going to be when he did?

A woman with long dark hair and a flowing skirt wheeled into the room. 'What's happening?' she asked, thankful for the diversion.

'Watch and see,' Taj said beside her, not relinquishing his hold on her.

The woman held her arms over her head and spun in front of them, her long hair flying and the layers of her skirt floating in her wake as she moved to the music. No, Morgan corrected herself. She didn't just move to the music, she was an extension of it. Like poetry, her hips circled. Back arched, head thrown back, her body performed a sensual rendition to music that was as powerful as it was beautiful. And while the dancer was demurely dressed, and there was nothing overtly erotic or even suggestive about the dance, Morgan found it impossible not to be moved by the sheer emotion of the performance. On some primitive level the music and the dance worked a charm of seduction, a power that increased as the dancer gained momentum, spinning and wheeling in a frenzy of movement, so expressive, so passionate.

'It's beautiful,' she said, unable to take her eyes from her as the dancer moved with grace and elegance, every part of her imbued with hidden meaning.

'It is the dance of love,' Tajik whispered close to her ear, his warm breath fanning her face, sending nerve-endings tingling. 'She is sending us on our way with a wish for pleasure, passion, and many fine sons.'

Breath caught in her throat as his words caught in her mind. *Many fine sons?* So now he intended her to be some kind of brood mare? She spun round, but immediately lost track of her protest. His face was right there, too close, his lips just millimetres from her own. Oh, God, she thought, her body already half alight, what the hell did she do now?

The music rose to a crescendo, crashing to a finale, and Morgan knew that behind her the dancer had finished her performance. But it was Taj who held her attention. Taj who took her hand in his and pressed it to his warm, sensual lips.

'Come,' he said. 'It is time.'

# CHAPTER EIGHT

UNDER a blanket of stars, and with a procession of guests and musicians accompanying them behind, they were carried aloft on a litter along the pathway to Tajik's quarters. Every bump and jostle escalated the already heady friction between them. The fabric between them meant nothing. Morgan knew she could be wearing full body armour and still she would be able to feel this man's heat, feel his want seeping through to her.

Torches lit the surrounds of the building, set at the top of a rise. Below them she could see similar torches, lighting the paths and buildings like fireflies. And beyond them was darkness lit only by the glowing moon and the blanket of stars above, as the desert and the night sky merged into one.

The carriers lowered their burden to the ground and Taj stepped off, taking her hand and leading her past two guards through ornately panelled doors into the interior. Cheers and song erupted from outside as the procession turned and headed back to the palace to continue the celebrations.

Morgan walked across the room, clutching her arms around her while Tajik closed the doors behind them and dimmed the lighting. She glanced around, trying to appreciate the magnificence of the space, with its light-coloured walls festooned with colourful Persian carpets echoing those covering the floor, its wide coffee tables laden with fruit, deep sofas with tasselled cushions and a central pole from which was suspended a canopy of fabric for a ceiling.

She'd barely registered it all when she jumped, feeling his hands on her shoulders, his face dipping close to her ear. 'So much more civilised than a tent, wouldn't you say?'

'It's beautiful,' she agreed, trying to calm her racing heart, wishing she weren't quite so jumpy, but wondering how, under the circumstances, she had any choice.

'Like you,' he said, turning her around in his arms, holding her there while his eyes drank her in. 'Beautiful. A vision in gold. Simply magnificent.'

She could barely breathe as he studied her face, his eyes intense, his mouth set. His fingers coaxed her chin higher, his touch triggering wave after wave of sensation spiralling deep down below.

'So beautiful,' he uttered on a breath, and his lips dipped lower, meeting hers in one sweet joining.

Part of her melted then and there, as his lips moved over hers in a sensual dance that transformed trepidation into anticipation. Her body, so keenly kept on tenterhooks tonight, hummed into life, even though he had barely touched her.

He broke the kiss and she looked up at him, knowing she was flushed and her breathing was already unsteady, knowing that he would take it as some kind of victory. But it didn't matter. Because his breathing was already ragged too, his nostrils flaring while the embers in his eyes sizzled and flared. And that gave her a sense of victory—that she could provoke such a reaction in such a powerful man.

Was it merely lust? Or did he feel something for her, his sheikha? Although why should she even care, another part of her mind insisted, if she was so set to bail out at the first opportunity that arose?

He touched a hand to her robe, slipping the first catch free, and her question shrank in relevance—the entire world shrank in relevance as what he was doing here and now, unfastening the heavy wedding robe, reigned supreme.

He took hold of both lapels and pushed the sides over her shoulders, letting the weight of her beautiful gown take it heavily to the floor. She should have tried to save it—she should have picked it up—but her attention was snagged by his intake of breath, the hiss of air between his teeth as he contemplated her in that diaphanous slip and the sheer underwear beneath. His eyes lit up like fires.

'Murjanah, you are more than any mere mortal could wish for.'

She closed her eyes. His words were like a caress to her soul—a caress she didn't want in case she started to believe him—in case he weakened her resolve.

'Don't talk,' she pleaded, her voice tighter than she'd ever known it. 'Just make love to me.'

He made a sound low in his throat, a growl, and collected her up in his arms so tenderly, as if she were something delicate and breakable rather than flesh and bone, and the fabric between her skin and his hands set a kind of electricity skittering through them as he walked.

Then he laid her down again in another room, on another bed. How many beds was it now that she had lain on with this man? And yet this time, she knew for a fact, the bed would be different. This time he would finish what he had started, soothe the ache building deep within her probably from the very first time they'd met.

He left her lying there, golden slippers on her feet and in a translucent robe that hid nothing, while, without taking his eyes from her, he wrenched off his headdress and shucked off his own robe.

His other clothes were similarly dispensed with, but he took his time this time, his actions purposeful and not urgent, as his actions had seemed to her last night.

He'd promised to be tender, but right now she wished he'd hasten—before she came to her senses and before he could deprive her of the completion she so craved. A need for completion only this man had ever inspired.

And then finally he was naked, and it was her turn to gasp, her turn to utter a feminine purr of appreciation, a sound that turned his mouth into a smile and further firmed that part of him that made him unmistakably male.

'Do not do that,' he warned her, 'when we need to take this slowly.'

Right now she didn't want slow. She just wanted him. Taj.

*Right now.*

Her body screamed it from every pore—so much so that when he slipped off her sequined shoes and started to caress her feet she almost howled with frustration.

He laughed as her head rammed back into the pillows, his five o'clock shadow a sensual rasp against the skin of her soles. 'Be patient, my little pearl. Your time is coming.'

He started there, caressing her toes and her feet, her soles and her heels, running his fingers over every surface, massaging every crook of bone and muscle, every tiny indentation. Then he started on her legs, pushing up the silken fabric as he went, and Morgan wanted to cry out in protest. The scars that he hadn't noticed last night in the full bloom of passion were too young, too raw to be missed by such an intensive exploration.

She knew the instant he found them—the marks from the screws that had held her shattered bones splinted together—the marks that remained red and shiny and as unsexy as hell.

He stilled and she held her breath, waiting for him to recoil, to decide she wasn't the woman he'd expected. And then, when instead of pulling back, he touched a finger to one shiny mound, caressing it gently.

'This is where they put the bolts that held your bones together?' he asked, before shifting his fingers to another scar higher up, and then another, before examining the other side of her leg. 'And these too?'

She nodded, too afraid to speak, the painful memories of how those marks had come about piling onto an already intensely emotional time. But, strangely, she was more afraid that suddenly he would find her unattractive and a poor choice of wife.

But then his lips dipped to that scarred skin, pressing to it gently. 'I give thanks to these marks,' he said, as he lowered his mouth to the next circle, kissing that too, and then the next and the next, kissing each of them in turn. 'As I give thanks to the surgeons who saved this glorious leg.'

Morgan battled not to let the tears fall. He didn't have to be so considerate. He didn't have to pretend that he cared. After all, against her will he had literally taken her for his wife. It was hardly as if this was some honeymoon scenario where the mood was meant to be romantic.

And yet it was as if he valued her in spite of her scarred leg—as if it made no difference to him that she wasn't as perfect as he'd thought.

But before she could form the words to signal her appreciation his lips had moved higher up her thigh, and all thought of rational conversation was burnt up in the heat generated by his mouth.

His teeth nipped at her skin, his tongue weaving a wicked path higher as he pushed up the gossamer-thin fabric before him. Fingers worked under the sides of her underwear, easing it down and away, and she wondered if he had changed his mind about going slow.

But then he lifted himself up her body, to pull her bodily into a kiss that rocked her senses. Somehow he manoeuvred her bra undone, and that too was skilfully dispensed with, leaving only a whisper of fabric between their heated nakedness.

He filled her mouth with heat and richness, an exotic blend of passion and masculine spice, and he filled one hand with her hair, the other with a breast that firmed and peaked under his ministrations. He dipped his mouth and through the fabric circled that tight bud with his tongue, causing an ache so deep she wanted to cry out with need.

Then he took her breast into his mouth, setting her body alight. His hand stroked her through the robe, the fabric slipping and tugging and setting up a delicious friction between their bodies that only added to the existing electricity.

He turned his attentions to her other breast, and her feelings of wanting him, *needing him*, intensified. She could feel him ready against her leg, hard and pulsing.

*Waiting.*

As she too was waiting.

But, as he'd promised, Taj was determined to take his time—to make love to her in the way she so properly deserved.

Did she deserve such exquisite pleasure when she had no intention of staying? Did she deserve such pleasure when, as soon as this night was over, her thoughts would once again turn to escape?

She gasped in air as his mouth moved lower, planting kisses over her abdomen, and then lower still. Right now there was no escape from his heated exploration of her body. And right now she was afraid she'd turn escape down if it were offered. For her senses and her body screamed for release from the mounting tension, release from the exquisite torture he was inflicting upon her with his mouth and his hands and every part of him.

And then he parted her most intimate folds, and shock turned to rapture as he made love to her through the sheer fabric with his mouth and tongue, stoking up the fires inside her, building an all-consuming need.

Her hips moved of their own accord, writhing under his skilful mouth in spite of herself. All she wanted was him inside her—knew it was necessary to complete this powerful circuitry. She tugged at his shoulders, fearing for herself, feeling herself losing touch with reality, being carried higher, as his tongue worked some kind of black magic and kept right on working despite her desperate efforts.

It came with a hitch of breath and a moment of sheer clarity. *She was lost*—before she came apart, her body shattering into pieces that drifted on the four winds over the desert sands, weightless and replete.

She lay there panting for air, her body humming as she

came back together. 'So glorious,' he said, kissing her softly on the mouth as he pulled her into his arms. She tasted herself on his lips as she wound her arms around his neck, feeling as supine and cosy as a cat soaking up the sun.

'Thank you,' she purred, wondering what people normally said under such circumstances, wanting to say something after what he'd done for her.

'That was just the entrée,' he said, his voice a wicked rumble against her throat as he tumbled her beneath him again, positioning himself between her legs. 'Now it's time for the main course.'

She gasped when she felt him pressing against her, afraid once again that he would be too much for her while at the same time her body welcomed his presence.

'Do not fear,' he soothed, 'you are more than ready.'

And so she held onto him and relaxed, trusting his knowledge of her as he tested her gingerly.

She doubted she could ever experience anything as mind-blowing as what he'd just done to her, but already she could see that there was a whole new world of sensations yet to explore. Already her muscles were trying to claim him as he gently stretched her more and more. Control was etched on his features. Sweat glowed on his brow and lined his back as he held himself in check. In check for her, she knew. Out of consideration for her.

And then, in one fluid stroke, he was inside her, and wonderment became her new watchword.

He stayed there, lodged deep inside her, his eyes fixed on hers, as if gauging how she was coping, before, obviously satisfied, he withdrew as slowly as he'd arrived. Loss seized her. She wanted more of that incredible feeling of fullness. And then with one steady thrust he drove home again, and she discovered that this was even better.

Slowly he built up the pace, encouraging her to match his movements, his golden eyes never leaving hers, his features intent with the effort he was exercising over his own body.

So she went with his rhythm, angling her hips to take him deeper, clamping down to hold him tight, even when his pace turned frantic. It was like climbing a mountain, with each stroke taking her higher towards the peak, a peak that seemed unattainable as her head thrashed on the pillow.

And then she was there, once again hovering on that desperate brink. She opened her eyes and saw him watching her, his face a study in concentration, as if he too was at that point of no return.

He lunged into her with a roar of triumph and sent her toppling over the edge, his cry in her ears as her world was torn apart.

He followed her, finding his own release, then collapsed partly over her, his head buried in the pillow alongside.

She lay there, her breathing steadying, her heartbeat slowly returning to normal.

He had no business making love to her like that—*as if he actually cared!*—when in fact he'd stolen her away from her sister and her family as if it was his God-given right with not a lick of regret. A family she didn't know when she might see again. A family who knew nothing of this sham of a marriage.

Little Ellie's plump features appeared in her mind's eye, bringing a brief smile to her face. Babies changed so fast. How old would Ellie be the next time she saw her? Would she even remember her? Fat tears started rolling down her cheeks.

She sniffed, clamping down on any idea that she would never see her tiny niece again. She would move heaven and earth to ensure that she did. And the sooner the better.

Taj could not be allowed to get away with what he had done.

No, she would not think more kindly of him simply because he was a generous and thoughtful lover. She would not!

He stirred alongside her, lifting himself up on one elbow. She turned her face away, trying to swipe away her tears, but he sat up at once.

'Murjanah?' he said, his voice heavy with concern. 'Is it your leg? Did I hurt you?'

She shook her head, fearful of talking in case she broke into sobs, but unable to stem the moisture seeping from her eyes. Her leg did ache—she was as much to blame as him for that—but it was nothing to the ache in her heart right now. It would have been easier if he *had* hurt her.

But he hadn't hurt her at all. In fact it had been a revelation, the most wondrous thing she'd ever experienced. And she'd remember it always as something special, even long after she'd left.

He kissed her softly on the lips. 'I have a surprise for you—a wedding gift. Maybe this will cheer you up.' He lifted an ornate box from the side-table and held it out to her.

He was giving her a gift? She scooted into a sitting position, covering herself as best she could with the translucent robe, thankful for even that amount of coverage. Taj, on the other hand, seemed totally at ease with his nakedness.

'It's beautiful,' she said, tilting the low, wide box this way and that, watching how the intricate mother-of-pearl and brass inlaid design glowed in the light. It was a stunning piece, the work of master craftsmen, she could see. 'Thank you.'

'You're supposed to open it,' he urged with a wry grin.

Her eyes flicked up to his. There was more? 'But I have nothing for you.'

'On the contrary,' he said. 'You've just given me the most precious gift in the world.'

Heat rose like a tide in her face, and she dropped her eyes, turning her gaze back to the box.

With shaky fingers she worked the brass clip, releasing it and lifting up the lid.

The contents took her breath away. Nestled against white satin, it lay there like a pirate's treasure: a necklace of diamonds and precious stones from which was suspended a dozen or more drops of gems in more shapes and more colours than she'd ever seen in one piece of jewellery. And yet it worked—gloriously so.

'They are all the colours of the sapphire,' he told her.

She shook her head. 'I can't take this. It's too much.'

'You must,' he told her, unclipping it from its satin bed. The stones winked at her in the light as they jostled against each other. 'This is my gift to you as my bride. It cannot be too much.'

He placed the necklace around her neck, clipping it over her hair before running his hands around her neck to set it free. Then he settled back to survey the effect. 'Beautiful. I knew it would suit your colouring. Look in the mirror—see for yourself.'

Reluctantly she eased off the bed, padding across the richly carpeted floor to the mirror, aware that she was wearing little more than nothing.

A stranger stared back at her. A shameless woman with love-swollen lips and a necklace that must be worth a king's ransom. She touched a hand to the jewels. The gems lay cool against her skin, but glowed warm in the glass, their many facets sparkling in the light, their mood cheery and full of hope.

If only she felt the same way.

He came up behind her, his hands large and weighty on her shoulders, his breath heavy with the taste of love. 'Almost perfect, wouldn't you say?'

'Almost?'

His hands moved to the fastenings of her barely-there slip.

'What are you doing?' she asked, clutching the sides together at her waist, as if the translucent fabric provided any kind of protection at all.

'Look now,' he said, and he slipped the robe from her shoulders, letting it bunch where she had her arms anchored around her waist, exposing her bare breasts to the mirror. 'Now, *that*,' he added, looking at her reflection in the mirror, his voice husky and deep, 'is perfection.'

His words shivered through her. He must feel something for her, surely, to make her want to believe he cared, to make her think that she was in some way special to him?

'You must be tired, my little pearl.'

She shrugged half-heartedly, but once again he was showing how well he could read her body. Because he was right. The tiresome proceedings of the journey, then the preparations, the heady anticipation, the intense crucible of their lovemaking—all of it had taken its toll. Already she could feel the strong feeling of anticlimax slowing her mind and veins.

He'd scooped her up into his arms before she realised

what was happening. But instead of taking her back to the bed, he walked away.

'Where are you taking me?'

'You need a bath to relax you before you sleep. I will bathe you.'

She turned rigid in his arms, wanting him to put her down. 'I don't need anyone to bathe me!'

But her protest went unheeded and he carried her into the next room. Soft lighting illuminated a super-sized bathroom that looked as big as the living room of her apartment at home. But no wonder, she thought, when she saw the size of the bath. Set deep into the floor, the wide infinity bath had to be at least ten feet long and six feet wide. Lights illuminated the pool from below, their colours blending, merging, ever changing, reminding her of the necklace at her throat.

'The necklace?' she said, worried for it, knowing it had to be worth so much as to have to be treated with kid gloves.

'Fear not. Those stones will not dissolve.' He took her down some steps, taking her into the fragrant depths and laying her to rest on a submerged ledge. The water lapped at her breasts, warm and scented with oils that slipped over her tender skin like a balm. She leaned her head back over a headrest, feeling the restorative effects of the bath already. Maybe this hadn't been such a bad idea after all.

Then he started soaping her, and her panic rose anew. 'I can do that.'

'No,' he insisted, using his hands to settle her back. 'You have performed your functions more than adequately tonight. This is my way of giving thanks.'

'Adequately?' she asked, her teeth suddenly set tighter than bricks in a wall. 'You think I performed "adequately"?'

If he noticed her sarcasm he ignored it, giving his attention to soaping her arms and shoulders. What should have felt sensual and relaxing felt more like a slap in the face in the wake of his cold summation.

'More than adequately,' he repeated, soaping her belly, his thumbs making large circles over it as if he was worshipping it. 'You will make the perfect vessel for my heir.'

This time she sat up in a rush, water sluicing from her as she pushed his arms away.

'What heir?'

His eyes gleamed purposefully. 'The child that even now might have been conceived in your womb.'

'Is that what this marriage is all about? Providing you with heirs? Conceiving your sons?'

He shrugged, an easy motion that belied the concrete set of his jaw. 'It is but one necessary function of my queen—wouldn't you agree?'

Oh, God! She'd been so thick—knowing that this was a marriage of convenience and yet still talking herself into thinking that he must care for her, still being seduced by his fine words and powerful sensuality and precious gifts, when the whole time he'd merely wanted her for her womb. There was nothing caring about words like "necessary function" and "vessel".

'You don't want a woman,' she snapped at him, pushing herself away from the ledge, anxious to get out of the bath and hide herself away before he could read the disappointment in her features. 'You need a brood mare!'

'That's odd,' he said, ignoring her jibe. 'You seemed to have no objections earlier to the process of conceiving a child.'

That was because she'd imagined he'd been *making*

*love*! But his latest words stung like bullets as she hauled herself up the steps.

'Come, Murjanah,' he reasoned from behind her, his voice less argumentative. 'You need to relax. Stay.'

But she didn't stay, and he made no attempt to stop her.

'My name is Morgan,' she flung over her shoulder as she climbed from the bath and buried herself in the folds of a thick robe. 'And I think I've had more than enough.'

# CHAPTER NINE

'YOU have to help me.'

It was during lunch the next day. The men had ridden out early to go hunting, streaming across the dunes, robes flapping in their wake, and it had taken Morgan this long to track down the Australian woman in the sea of women chattering away in the banquet hall.

Sapphy's eyes instantly filled with concern. 'Of course I'll do anything I can. What's the problem?'

Morgan looked around, making sure no one was in earshot. 'I have to get home. Can you get me out of here?'

Sapphy tilted her head. 'You mean home to Australia? But why? Whatever's happened?'

'I shouldn't be here at all. I thought I was coming to be Nobilah's companion, but it was a trick. Once I was here, Taj calmly informed everyone we were married. I had no choice…' Morgan trailed off, biting her lip, too close to tears to continue.

'Oh, Morgan.' Sapphy took her hand. 'I knew it had all happened quickly, but I thought Taj had fallen in love with you at first sight. He is clearly besotted with you—anyone can see that.'

Morgan squeezed her eyes shut and shook her head. She'd

given up on that particular fantasy last night, when Taj had so pragmatically brought home her real purpose here.

'And you feel nothing for him?'

*Not any more.* 'How can I? He wants me for my breeding capabilities. Nothing else.'

'He said that?'

'As good as! Listen, Sapphy, you have to help me escape. You have to help me get somewhere where I can find an Australian embassy and get home. I don't know who else to turn to.'

The other woman leaned back, her expression grim. 'Morgan, I don't know if it's as easy as that. Taj and Khaled are very close. If I did something against Taj I can't imagine what the ramifications might be.'

'But I can't stay here. I just *can't*!'

Sapphy frowned. 'He hasn't been violent with you, has he? I wouldn't have thought Taj capable of it, but if he's hurt you in any way…'

She shook her head. Passionate—yes. Tender—yes. But he hadn't been anywhere near violent. Even this morning, when she'd made it clear she was not interested in making love, he hadn't forced himself on her as she'd half expected of the desert ruler. He'd merely dressed and taken himself off with a simple kiss to her turned-away cheek. 'No, nothing like that. It's just all wrong. I have to escape!'

Abir came up to them, carrying a coffee jug and a platter of sweetmeats, and Sapphy warned silence with her eyes until the girl had moved on. Then she squeezed Morgan around the shoulders. 'I do understand. And, believe me, I know more than most what it's like to feel trapped. But I have to point out the difficulties. It will not be easy. But it could be done if we are very careful.'

Morgan felt the tiny glimmer she'd felt when she'd first met her compatriot burst into the bright flame of hope.

'You really will help me?'

Sapphy took hold of both her hands. 'Yes, of course I will. But first you must be absolutely certain. Believe me, Arab males are sometimes not the best communicators when it comes to matters of the heart, and they have a reputation for some unorthodox courting techniques, so it's easy to misinterpret their emotions.'

'I'm absolutely certain. He lost his fiancée twelve months ago, and his heart is still filled with her. There is no place for me.'

Sapphy nodded, her eyes sad. 'I remember hearing news of the accident. It was a terrible time for everyone—Taj especially. But please don't give up on him just yet.' The woman took a deep breath and pressed her lips together. 'I tell you what—we're here for two weeks of celebration, so to do anything before we're due to leave would be madness, but if you still feel the same way two weeks from now then I promise I will find a way to take you with us and get you home.'

'Don't worry,' Morgan told her. 'I'll be coming with you.'

Sapphy tilted her head, her expression quizzical. 'You know, I'm not making light of your claims, but you remind me so much of me a little while after I arrived in Jebbai. I couldn't wait to get away.'

Morgan frowned. 'But you're still here. What happened?'

'I fell in love with Khaled. That's what happened.'

'But that's different. Khaled loves you. I saw the way he held you at the banquet last night.'

'He does, that's true, but things were not always so clear. That's why I'm suggesting you see how things go.

Taj is a good man. I've known him almost as long as I've known Khaled. But these men are strong willed. Sometimes they don't recognise what they feel, no matter what they tell themselves—or tell their women, for that matter.'

'You're telling me there's a chance that Taj might actually feel something for me beyond wanting a handy breeding ground for his children?'

'Looking at you two together last night, I'd be very surprised if he doesn't already. Maybe with time he will realise it himself, and you will believe it too, and change your mind about leaving. While I understand your reasons for wanting to leave, if you leave now you'll never know.'

Morgan shook her head. Sapphy had obviously been lucky, but her circumstances were no doubt vastly different from her own. 'No,' she said, 'I won't change my mind.'

Sand and dust were everywhere—an endless irritation as the party ate up the dunes on their way back to the palace, several gazelle and many smaller game richer than when they'd begun their quest. Their catch would make a great feast. All in all, it had been a good day.

Hopefully Taj's new wife felt the same way. She had been decidedly frosty this morning when he had left, and he had allowed her space. He understood she might be tender, but he had done all he could last night to ease her way into the manners of love. But eventually she would have to understand that he was just a man, that he couldn't be patient too much longer.

Especially not when he knew what pleasures were in store. She was a beauty, his Murjanah. More spirited than he'd ever imagined, she was a beauty inside and out—a rare find. His rare small pearl indeed.

To think that if Qasim had not plotted his betrothal to Abir he might have missed Murjanah's charms entirely. The thought brought a smile to his face as he contemplated his reaction. He would have to remember to thank Qasim.

Thoughts of last night's lovemaking played through his mind, turning him hard in the saddle. She'd been such a quick study. For someone so apparently inexperienced in the ways of love, she'd responded to his moves as if she was born to them, her body a natural complement to his own. And with the eagerness she'd displayed in receiving his attentions, it would be only a matter of time before she began to practise her own talents.

What little moisture there was in this sun-dried atmosphere evaporated fast in his throat. He could hardly wait.

Despite the challenge they'd faced during the long day, and the steady pace of his team, he urged his horse still faster over the dunes. He needed to get back.

Finally the palace and the tent city behind it came into view. He jumped from the saddle, throwing the reins to one of the boys with instructions to look after his horse, and then set off to his villa.

He found her lying down, her face averted, on a table on the private deck, her beautiful back bare and glistening with oil as a masseuse worked on her. He signalled silence to the woman and let himself noiselessly into the house, wanting to rid himself of the scent of horse and desert before he greeted his wife.

Five minutes later, showered and covered in a plush robe, he let himself out onto the deck once more, signalling for the woman to leave.

She bowed and complied, her fabric slippers making barely a sound as she departed, while he oiled his hands in readiness. Murjanah didn't move, oblivious to the switch.

Below him her skin gleamed like a million pearls, lustrous and inviting. Her buttocks were hidden for now under a towel, their soft rounded shape like a call to action. Part of him was too polite to refuse.

All day he had been waiting for this. All day he had been looking forward to the time when once again his hands could be upon her. But never in his wildest fantasies had he imagined that fate would deliver him his wish in so delightful a way.

She felt like warm silk under his hands, soft and smooth. He spread his fingers out and traced up the line of her spine with his thumbs, massaging her shoulders and neck gently before returning to her waist and repeating the movement up her spine.

'Mmmm,' she purred. 'That feels good.'

He smiled to himself, not about to disagree.

Sapphy had been right, thought Morgan, as she felt her tension disappearing under the skilful hands of the masseuse. The other woman had convinced her that a massage would relax her and enable her to think more clearly. She wasn't sure she needed to think more clearly—she'd made up her mind to leave, and no amount of thinking was going to sway her on that point—but it was certainly relaxing. She could feel the tension of the last few days sliding away. And it didn't hurt at all that Taj was out for the day and not expected back much before sunset.

Fingertips brushed against the curve of her breast as they ascended her spine, sending a faint shiver through her. Her body seemed so sensitive after Taj's lovemaking last night.

One mere gliding touch of a masseuse setting her off. Fingers brushed against her again and her breasts tingled in response.

Memories, she told herself. It was memories of last night that made her so receptive to touch, made her breasts continue to hum.

Thankfully the masseuse's hands moved lower, spanning her back at her waist, thumbs moving in lazy circles in the small of her back, slowly dipping lower, inching down the towel that covered her behind until it was completely exposed.

She tried to stay cool. So they did things a little differently here? That was no surprise. Re-oiled hands met the globes of her behind, alternately squeezing and massaging, doing wicked things to her pulse-rate.

Somewhere along the line this massage had gone from being relaxing to downright erotic.

'Thank you,' she said, lifting her head from the pillow. 'I think that's enough for now.'

'At least for this side,' he said.

She jerked around, grabbing for the towel at her rear at the same time, but he'd already moved it out of reach. 'How…?'

He smiled. 'Turn over.'

She blinked, and he repeated the instruction. 'I'm not finished yet,' he added.

Her body tingling, a mass of nerves, she turned face up on the table, knowing that every part of her was blushing red to his gaze.

'Such perfection,' he uttered like a growl as he surveyed her, oiling his hands. 'The only dilemma is where to start?'

In the end he did as he'd done last night, and started with her feet, moving up each leg so slowly and thoroughly that she thought she would scream under his masterful hands.

Desire coiled like a living thing inside her, infusing her veins with a primitive need, plumping her in readiness.

But, while the power of her response surprised her, she rationalised that lust didn't change anything. She would still flee the first chance she had. Maybe it was better to go along with him and let him think she was compliant, lest he become suspicious. Better to let him think she was falling under his spell.

Somewhere along the way his robe had fallen open. He had left it that way, so that she could make no mistake about his own arousal. He was so large, it seemed impossible. But she knew now that she could accommodate him. Indeed, she physically ached to do so.

Once again he must have read her mind. He took hold of her calves, careful to avoid pressing on her scars, and slid her bodily down towards the end of the table. He ran his hands along the length of her legs and lifted them over his shoulders.

'I have looked forward to this moment all day,' he told her, his expression intense as he found her slick core and pressed himself home.

Her body seemed to purr with relief. But only for an instant. Because there was no relief. Already primed by his magic hands, her body was building quickly. A second lunge followed the first, then a third, lifting her higher and ever higher until she went shattering into her climax.

She took him with her, pulling him over the abyss, sending him pumping his release into her before he collapsed, heaving, over her.

Languid and feeling boneless, this time she let him carry her to the bath with no protest. This time she let him soap her and wash her and then make love to her all over again.

And all the while she told herself that, even if it was good sex, good sex changed nothing.

Sapphy met up with her in the hallway at dinner that night. 'That necklace is fantastic,' she said. 'Did Taj give it to you?'

Morgan nodded. Taj had told her to wear it tonight, and Morgan had felt some of her old resentment seep back in the wake of their lovemaking. Or, more fittingly, *baby-making*, she had reminded herself as she'd fixed her necklace at the throat.

The trophy wife wearing the trophy necklace.

'It's so beautiful,' Sapphy continued. 'But it's not just the necklace. You seem so much more relaxed tonight. Did you have that massage, like I suggested?'

Morgan signalled her assent, trying to withhold the blush that wanted to accompany the memory. 'It was—*better* than I expected,' she confessed, finding it hard to meet the other woman's gaze. If she admitted how she'd spent the latter part of her afternoon to Sapphy, then she'd no doubt assume all her troubles were over. And they weren't.

Because fundamentally nothing had changed. Taj had still basically kidnapped her to provide him with an heir and however many spares, and she'd be damned if she'd let herself stay hijacked by anyone.

Beside her, Sapphy smiled and squeezed her hand as they walked back from the ladies' lounge. 'I'm glad to see you looking so refreshed. Do you think you can make it through the next two weeks all right, while you decide?'

'I have decided,' she said. 'I'm leaving.'

But for the first time she didn't experience the secret thrill that had accompanied that concept before.

It's only sex, she told herself as, back inside the banquet

hall, she sat down alongside Taj and felt the magnetic pull of his body heat once more. *It's only sex.*

'Having a nice chat with your compatriot?' Taj asked her.

Morgan sneaked a sideways look at him. Did he suspect something was up? 'Yes, thanks. It's nice to talk to someone who speaks my language.'

'*I* speak your language,' he growled, his eyes clearly unpleased.

'I mean she understands me.'

'You think I don't?' He touched his fingers to her arm, tracing a line upwards to her neck and cheek, setting off a tremor that moved like a chain reaction through her flesh. His eyes held her prisoner. 'I know what you need.' His voice rumbled through her, 'I know what you want.'

'Is that so?' she challenged, already feeling her body preparing itself for another of his sensual onslaughts. Already delighting in the anticipation of what would come later. 'And what is it that I want?'

He let his hand fall, seemingly innocuously, and yet managed to brush one straining nipple through her robe with the back of his hand on the way down. By design? She couldn't help but believe so.

He smiled. 'You want me.'

Her heart thudded hard in her chest. But still somehow she managed to turn on her coolest look for him. One thing she wouldn't miss after she'd gone was his unbridled arrogance. 'You're very sure of yourself, aren't you?'

'Just as I am sure of you.'

Don't bet on it, she thought, turning her eyes away and feigning interest in the tray of food she was being offered.

*Don't bet on it.*

# CHAPTER TEN

S<small>HE</small> made the discovery the next morning.

'What's wrong?' Taj asked, coming up behind her as she searched through the wide bathroom vanity unit.

'Nothing's wrong,' she snapped, looking over her shoulder, thinking her privacy had gone the same way as her freedom—a thing of the past. Nothing *was* wrong— in fact everything couldn't be more perfect. The last thing she needed was a baby on board when she fled the country. Now there was next to no chance she'd conceive before she escaped. 'I've got my period, that's all.'

He stood taller in his long navy bathrobe. 'So that explains your snippiness of the last day or two?'

'If you say so,' she responded drily. 'Though it could have something to do with being tricked into coming to Jamalbad and being forced to marry you.'

He took her by the shoulders, turning her fully around to meet his frown.

'You are not happy here?'

'That's hardly the point! Where do you get off, holding people against their will to become your personal incubator?'

'I haven't noticed you fleeing from my bed!'

She shrugged, turning her eyes away and wondering if she was overplaying her hand. The last thing she wanted to do was give him any idea of what she had planned.

'How long,' he continued, 'will your period last?'

'Four days—maybe five.'

'Then, if it pleases you, I will not bother you for sex for five nights,' he continued.

'Why would you bother, I suppose,' she snapped back, 'when there's no chance of the conception of your immaculate heir?'

He stared at her a second. 'Now, that is interesting,' he said. 'I had thought not to inconvenience you during this time, but now I wonder if perhaps you might be more inconvenienced by my abstinence? Are you disappointed, my little pearl? You have been such an avid student of the art.'

She shrugged carelessly once more. 'I guess the sex is okay.'

His hand pulled her chin around in time for her to see his eyes narrow, his nostrils flaring. She could see she'd scored a direct bull's-eye with her insult.

'It's "okay"?'

'Well, how would I know how you rate? I haven't exactly had a wealth of experience.'

'And what was wrong with your fiancé that this is so?'

She swallowed, her mouth suddenly dry as she realised she'd once foolishly held up her engagement to Evan as some kind of defence. 'Who said there was something wrong with him?'

'There must have been, surely, for him not to want to make love to you.'

She squeezed her eyes shut. 'Maybe he just wanted to wait until we were married. You did yourself.'

'How long were you engaged?'

'Two years.'

He smiled, all too knowingly. 'Then he was no man at all. Because a real man couldn't wait. Not for a prize such as you.'

'It's history,' she stated, wanting to change the topic before she could read too much into his words. She'd done that before—had hoped it meant he was softening towards her—and it only cost her more when he reminded her of her true purpose here. 'If it makes you feel any better, I guess that means you're my best so far. Does that help?'

His arms rammed down either side of her, pinning her to the vanity. 'I am your best—*ever*!'

She swallowed. 'I'll have to keep you posted on that score.'

He wheeled away, cursing in his own language.

'Does it mean *nothing* to you that of all the women in the world I chose *you* to be my bride? I chose *you* to be the mother of my children?'

'And I'm supposed to be flattered? When you have wrenched me away from my life and my family?'

'I will give you family!'

It was suddenly all too much. Too much tension. Too much drama. 'What part of this don't you understand? I want my *own* family! I want to see my sister and my brother-in-law, and my baby niece before she's grown up and completely forgotten who I am. I want to know that I will see them again and not be stuck here alone for ever!'

Her voice cracked on the last word and she spun away, clutching her arms around herself. Tears clouded her vision, but she was unwilling to let him see how much she hurt, how deep was her pain.

Tegan would be worried sick about her. Morgan hadn't had a chance to drop her twin a line—not even a hint to let her know she had arrived and was still alive, even if things had not gone completely to plan.

Then she felt his long arms wrap around her, holding her to him in a warm embrace, his lips dipping to her head.

'You love this sister very much.'

Morgan sniffed. 'Of course I love her! She's my twin. Along with Maverick and baby Ellie she's all I have in the world.'

He turned her slowly in his arms to face him, shaking his head. 'No—now you have me. And soon you will have a child of your own. But I will see what I can do about having your sister and her family visit.'

She looked up at him suspiciously while tears clumped her lashes into spikes, too afraid to believe him, too afraid not to. 'You'd do that?'

'I want you to be happy here,' he said, pressing his lips gently to her own. 'I will do anything to make it so.'

It was true, he realised some time later, as he walked his steed alongside his wife's chosen mount. At the time it had been a throwaway comment, but when her face had lit up when he'd suggested having her family to visit, he'd known then and there that he wanted to see her smile at him like that more often. He wanted her to be happy. And maybe, he recognised, there were more things he could do to make her journey into becoming his sheikha more bearable.

He would talk to Kamil to arrange things. He would make it happen.

The sun beat down on them, harsh and unforgiving, though it was barely eleven in the morning and their ride was almost over. She'd insisted on coming out with him, saying that she wanted a break away from the palace and the endless chatter of a thousand women, convincing him that her leg was up to a gentle ride through the dunes to a nearby oasis, but it was clear the unfamiliar exercise was more taxing than she'd imagined. Under the rim of her hat he could see her face was pale and sweat streaked, and every now and her jaw would clench and he could almost feel her pain.

'Come,' he said, drawing his mount closer. 'take my arm. Ride with me.'

'I can manage,' she said through gritted teeth.

'Save your leg,' he urged. 'Come.'

Reluctantly, she acquiesced. She hated showing him she was weak in any way, but she hadn't ridden since the accident, and the ache in her lower leg and knee was reaching screaming pitch. And with the endless heat...

He circled her waist with his arm and hauled her from the saddle, swinging her across in front of him as if she weighed nothing at all, even though his steed stood several hands higher than her pretty mare. She collapsed against his firm torso, grateful right now for his strength and power, relishing it as the pain in her leg started to abate, settling into a throb.

He brought her in with one arm to keep her close, covering her face with his robe to protect her from the sun now that she had removed her hat. 'Is that more comfortable?'

'Thank you,' she said, rubbing her cheek against his chest as she snuggled in, drinking in the marvellous scent of this man—sandalwood, spice and testosterone rolled into one seductive package. A package that was suddenly all the more attractive with his seeming change of heart this morning.

He would arrange for her sister and family to visit her. Even now the thrill of that news overrode the remaining pain of her aching leg. It was news that had blindsided her. He had sounded so earnest, so sincere, and she had no doubt he would make it happen. Part of her wanted to think he must care for her after all, to go to such lengths to make her happy.

Maybe Sapphy had been right. These men operated under a different framework, used to ruling on high and having their every command obeyed. Communicating their emotions was perhaps not their strongpoint. But Taj showed snippets of humanity she would never have believed him of possessing earlier.

Morgan was learning more about her new husband all the time—that his tenderness was not an accident or a ruse, and that he was a powerful man who could also be gentle and caring.

And Taj seemed finally to be starting to understand her needs—and not just her body's needs, which he was more than enough to assuage, despite her taunts. For, while she was inexperienced, she'd read plenty in magazines and articles to know that he must be an exceptional lover. She didn't need real-life comparisons to conclude that.

She snuggled deeper into his robes, anchoring herself against his chest as the horse padded over the sand. If she did leave, she would miss his strength and power and the feel of this hard body. And, if she was totally true to herself, she would probably miss the sex.

*Probably, nothing.* She would *definitely* miss the sex.

But physical pleasure was no reason to change her mind and stay, even when she considered the concession he'd belatedly made to her today to arrange for her sister to visit— a concession she wouldn't need if she had already fled, and a concession he might easily have made simply to ensure that she would not cause trouble for him.

It was too confusing. Where once she'd been so certain now she was wavering, and she wasn't even sure why. He'd still kidnapped her. He'd still insisted she marry him. By rights she should hate him for what he'd done. She'd once thought she did. And yet now she was thinking about giving it time before she decided whether she stayed or left.

*Why?*

She closed her eyes, letting the rhythm of the horse's movements rock her while lying sheltered in her warm cocoon, protected and cosseted. Nothing had to be decided today—Sapphy wouldn't be leaving for over a week.

By then she would know.

Tajik didn't make it easy for her. The next few days were a busy whirl of outings and adventures, and through it all he was the consummate host. Nothing was too much trouble. He saw to her every need.

She marvelled when he introduced her to his hunting falcons, with their powerful bodies and tiny masks. He showed her how they soared and wheeled and then dived for prey, supreme in the sky, supreme hunters. And she sensed in her heart that if Taj was a bird he would be a falcon, strong and supreme, and amongst the falcon numbers he would reign supreme.

Another day he took her by four-wheel drive to the nearby mountain range with its ragged peaks, just visible from the palace, and together they explored the pool-filled riverbeds, enjoying lunch together in the shade of palm trees deep inside one gorge.

'It's beautiful here,' she said. 'So peaceful and serene.'

He conceded the point, but added, 'Do not be taken in by these snaking riverbeds. Many a man has come to grief following their twisted path thinking they will lead him out of the mountains, when they have only led him to his death.'

She shivered, looking at the high walls of the gorge around them, wondering what it would be like to be lost and searching for a way out.

He wrapped her in his arms. 'With me,' he said, 'you need never fear. With me you will always be safe. Come, we have more things to explore.'

On the way back to the palace he took her to the ruins of an ancient fortress, long abandoned but rich with the memories of the desert years.

Another day she watched, enthralled, when all the men competed in an archery contest on the dunes beyond the tent encampment. And she found herself cheering alongside Sapphy when one after another the men bowed out, leaving only two men remaining in the competition: Taj and Khaled. They went arrow for arrow, until finally one of Khaled's arrows narrowly missed the mark.

He slapped his friend on the back as he conceded defeat with a smiled warning. 'Next time, my friend!'

Afterwards Taj let her try her hand. The traditional bow was heavy and awkward, even when Taj stood behind her, his lips at her ear, helping her to draw back the string. Her focus was not helped by his heated presence behind her, and thoughts of what she was missing out on, and her arrow failed to launch, dropping to the ground ineffectually. She laughed and swung round to hand back the bow, and then she saw his eyes, the fires flaring bright, and his look took her breath away. He, too, was waiting.

She wanted him, she admitted to herself later that day, as they sat out amongst the dunes for a starlit feast. It had been four nights of being spooned tightly against him, his hands caressing, soothing her to sleep, but tonight she was beyond caressing. Tonight her hunger would wait no more. Tonight her hunger demanded to be fed.

Under a backdrop of stars families and clans gathered around the glow of the fires, enjoying the feast of mezze dishes. Music wafted in and out on the desert breeze, the smell of spit-roast lamb and spices competing with the baked apple scent of the shisha pipes many of the men favoured smoking, the burble of the water adding a gentle sound to the air.

Morgan sipped on her sweet mint tea, watching a small herd of oryx wander through the groups, her senses humming. It was the most beautiful night, with everything she loved about Jamalbad right here—the colour, the character, and the sheer beauty of the desert and its people.

In just a few days she had started to feel at home in her new role, coming to terms with the respect of the women and their desire to please her as Taj's sheikha. And with the assistance of a tutor she was making her first tentative steps into learning the language, so she could communicate with them on their own terms.

Morgan breathed in the heady atmosphere and felt good. Beside her sat Taj, straight and tall. Nobilah sat nearby, as did Sapphy and Khaled, each with a small child on their lap, feeding them snippets of flat bread and dip.

They were beautiful children, their skin a light caramel, their features a blend of the best of both parents. And Sapphy glowed with pride. She was pregnant again, she'd told her excitedly that afternoon, and Morgan could see the happiness etched in her beautiful features. Her husband was clearly so proud of her at the news.

What would Taj's children look like? Would they share his golden eyes? Or would they have her everyday hazel ones? They would have his dark hair and beautiful skin, she was sure. She would want them to.

It was with a sizzling zip up her spine that she realised that for the first time she was actually contemplating having her captor's babies.

She looked over at Sapphy and her family. Could she be so lucky if she stayed? Could that be her fate? Taj had shown her a side of himself in the last few days that she couldn't help but be drawn to. They'd enjoyed so much together, even laughed together. It was no longer just physical.

And the thought of leaving him...

But the thought of seeing her twin and baby Ellie tugged at her too. She missed them so much. And Taj had not mentioned again the prospect of them visiting. Had he been serious? Or just trying to make her feel better at the time?

The man at her side finished his conversation with his neighbour, wrapping his arm around Morgan possessively. She nestled into his hard body, liking the way he preferred to keep her close.

'I have a surprise for you,' he said.

Her fingers went to the necklace at her throat—the necklace that marked her as his wife, *his woman*. 'You've already given me so much.'

'I think you will like this,' he said with a knowing smile. 'I have arranged for your sister and family to join us here in Jamalbad in late December. For your Christmas. They will stay for a month. More if you like.'

Her jaw dropped. She blinked twice. 'You're kidding me?'

He took her hand and pressed the back of it to her mouth. 'Apparently your sister is both amazed and delighted with your news.'

'You're actually serious?' She shook her head, sure she's misheard him. 'You really have spoken to Tegan?'

'Kamil has,' he corrected her. 'It is all his doing.'

'No,' she said, happiness bubbling up like a well inside her. 'Nothing happens here without your say-so. *You* have made it happen. Oh, thank you!' she squealed, throwing her arms around his neck. 'Thank you. Thank you. Thank you.'

He'd done this for her. He'd done this because he wanted her to be happy. Maybe, she thought, as his hold on her relaxed enough to slide down and let his lips find hers, maybe it was time to believe he did care for her—even just a little. His mouth moved over hers in a kiss that rocked her, tugging at her heart, opening it. Maybe it was time to believe that he truly had chosen her from that first moment as the woman he wanted to marry. Maybe it was time to believe he had sensed a connection even then.

And maybe... Maybe it was even time to believe she loved him? Before she'd finished the question, with heart-stopping realisation she knew it to be true. She loved Taj, heart and soul. She could no sooner leave him than stop breathing. He was part of her now—a part of her she could never live without.

Passion ignited like an electrical storm between them, days of abstinence fuelling the energy and the sparks.

It was Morgan who broke the kiss at last, her breathing as frantic and as choppy as his appeared to be. 'Make love to me,' she whispered. 'Make love to me tonight.'

* * *

It wasn't just sex. Lovemaking didn't do it justice. Frantically they reached for each other, wrenching clothes out of the way, discarding fragments of garments carelessly as they moved inexorably towards the bed. There was but one purpose to their actions, one goal.

And when they finally came together it was a conflagration, an inferno in which she felt her soul melded for ever with his.

He was beautiful, this Arab sheikh of hers. He was powerful and magnificent, and he carried the colour and character of the desert with him.

And as he took her higher she had not one doubt that he cared about her. In fact, she knew he must. Why else would he have done so much for her? Why else would he have gone so far out of his way to make her happy when he already had her captive here? He hadn't had to do that. Which meant he must love her too, just a little.

And even just a little, she decided, would be enough.

## CHAPTER ELEVEN

'I'M NOT coming with you.'

It was the last day before the celebrations were to end. Sapphy and Khaled and all the other tribespeople were due to leave. The sun was high in the sky, a herd of oryx were grazing casually nearby, and the two women were walking in the shade of a palm-lined promenade siding the palace, the sweet scent of ripe citrus filling the air.

Sapphy wheeled around and looked at her, her blue eyes sparkling, her cerulean abaya rippling in the light breeze. 'Do you mean what I think you mean?'

Morgan smiled wider—which was hard when it felt as if she'd been smiling all day. 'I honestly can't think of a time when I've been happier.' And it was true. Somehow the relaxed lifestyle of the desert kingdom had worked its way into her senses, unwinding her from that buttoned up PA she'd been and transforming her into someone who loved the freedom of the desert dress, freeing her from the support stockings to the feel of the desert wind in her hair. And without a doubt she knew the change had much to do with Taj and how he made her feel as a woman.

*As his woman.*

Sapphy squealed with joy and took both of Morgan's

hands in her own, her own smile wide and beaming. 'Then I'm over-the-moon happy for you. I knew something was up when I saw you two at the dinner the other night. You both looked so close—although I was still holding my breath, hoping it might work.'

'You were right to suggest I wait,' Morgan admitted. 'These last few days he's been so considerate, so kind. And since then I've seen you with Khaled and with your boys. I have to admit I want what you're having.'

Sapphy enclosed her in a hug. 'Seeing how happy you've been with Taj, I have no doubt you'll get it.'

Morgan returned the squeeze with one of her own. 'Thank you so much for being here, and for helping me out. Because I realise how much you were risking by promising to help me. I'm so glad to know I have a good friend just across the border.'

'Any time you need me,' Sapphy assured her, 'I'll be there.'

On a balcony set high atop the desert palace, the remaining family members watched their departing visitors as they streamed out into the desert. The tent city had been taken down and cleared, and now all that remained to be seen were the long caravans of heavily packed camels and brightly turned-out horses, all heading in different directions.

Morgan waved to the fleet of four-wheel drives heading back across the border to Jebbai, though she knew Sapphy would never see her from there. She might have been with them now, secreted away inside one of them, heading to freedom, had she decided not to stay.

How close she had come to giving it all away!

Nobilah sighed alongside them. 'Well, that's that, then. Tomorrow it's back to Jamalbad City for the rest of us.'

Morgan was feeling a little wistful herself. Their time here at the desert palace was something she'd remember always. She turned her head to look up at the golden-eyed man at her side. For here was the place where she'd fallen in love with her desert king.

He looked down at her and snagged her appreciative gaze, and they shared a smile that warmed her from the inside out, setting her senses tingling.

She was just turning to follow Nobilah inside when across the balcony she caught Qasim's eyes upon her. What she saw there curdled her blood. No longer merely simmering, it was raw hatred that radiated out across the space to her.

With a sneer that tilted his mouth, Qasim whispered something in the ear of the smoky-eyed girl alongside him before he shoved her inside the palace before him.

Morgan shivered and stopped, not wanting to be anywhere near the man. Why did he hate her so much? What had she ever done to him?

'Murjanah?' Taj said, his hand on her arm. 'Is something wrong?'

'It's Qasim—the way he looks at me. Like he hates me, or something. He's made it plain from the start he doesn't like me, but never have I seen him so angry as just now. What have I done to make him hate me so much?'

Taj frowned, his eyes following Qasim's progress into the palace. 'Qasim has had a recent disappointment that he takes too much to heart. Don't worry yourself about him. I will speak to him.'

'What kind of disappointment?'

'Nothing you need be concerned with. Leave it with me.'

Morgan was more than happy to. She headed off for one last walk in the orange grove with Nobilah, before returning to their suite to start thinking about packing.

She would miss this place. She would miss the gentle oryx and the spectacular sunrises and sunsets. But they would come back—maybe in December, when Tegan and her family visited? She would so love to share the wonders of this harsh but beautiful desert land with them. She would ask Taj if it was possible.

She let herself into the suite, surprised to see her husband standing immobile in the centre of the living room, almost as if he'd been waiting for her. She smiled automatically, already mouthing a greeting, then noticed the look of dark thunder that held his features rigid, the stance that saw his arms crossed over his chest like a stop sign.

'Taj?' she whispered, a feeling of *déjà-vu* overwhelming her as she feared a return to those first few days, where his passion had been played out in anger rather than love. 'What's wrong? Whatever's happened?'

His golden skin was underlined with fire. His jaw clicked. Finally he unhinged it enough to speak.

'What have you done with the necklace?'

Ice filled her veins. She hadn't known what to expect, but this was far and away out of left field. 'What are you talking about?'

'Have you forgotten already the necklace I bestowed upon you as a wedding gift?'

'Of course not. I just don't know what you're getting at. What about it?'

'Then—if you remember it—where is it?'

Fear snaked its way up her spine. Whatever was wrong, whatever he thought was wrong, somehow he believed she was implicated in it. The heady feelings she'd been experiencing these last few days started to sour. Surely she hadn't misjudged him that badly…?

'It's in the box,' she said unsteadily, already fearing the worst and more as she stated the obvious—the place he must already have checked. 'the box you gave me.'

'You mean this box?' he charged, picking up the hand-carved inlaid box from where it had been hidden on a coffee table behind him. 'This *empty* box?'

He brandished it before her, already open, the space where her necklace had once nestled a silent accusation.

She knew her mouth had fallen open, but she was powerless to prevent it, even though she'd already had warning that something was seriously wrong. She shook her head, collecting her senses. 'It was there this morning. I swear it.'

'And you don't know what happened to it?'

'Of course not! It was there. Right there!'

'So you didn't take the necklace in order to bribe someone to get you passage out of here?'

She blinked, her senses reeling. This was suddenly getting too dangerous—a lie that was perilously close to the truth. 'No! Absolutely not. Why would you even suggest it? I love that necklace.'

For the first time he seemed to relax. His head fell back on his shoulders. 'I knew he was lying—that you weren't capable of such deception. But when I came back here and found the necklace missing…'

He put the box down and came closer, dropping an arm

over her shoulder. 'I'm sorry, Murjanah. I should have trusted you.'

She looked into his eyes, searching for the truth. Was a simple denial enough to assuage his beliefs? 'Who told you I stole my own necklace?'

'It is not important. I will deal with it.'

'But don't you see? Maybe they know something. They must, to know it's gone—'

He pressed his lips to hers, quietening her as he drew her into his arms. It was warm there. Warm and familiar. And Morgan wanted above anything to believe that his mistrust of her was a mere glitch. He must realise how much she was concerned with the disappearance. He must know she was innocent.

'I will find the necklace,' he assured her, pressing his lips to her hair. 'What is important for me now is that I realise all the rest I heard must also be lies.'

She stilled, silently praying. Surely there couldn't be more? 'What else was there?'

'It's nothing, I'm sure. Just another ridiculous accusation that involved one of our esteemed guests.'

Morgan went rigid in his arms and immediately wished she hadn't—in case he read her body language as well as he maintained. Right now, with the necklace missing, was not the time to admit that she had indeed been planning to escape but had changed her mind. And the necklace theft had been a lie. Why should this piece of information be any different?

'And what did they say?'

He shrugged. 'Merely that you were both overheard in conversation, plotting your departure from Jamalbad.'

Ice filled her veins.

*Someone knew!*

But who could have overheard them? Unless… She thought back to when she'd first spoken to Sapphy—they'd been lunching together, and Abir had come over with a tray. Could it be the girl who had overheard them? Who else could it be?

While fear chilled her extremities, panic instilled a tremor in her voice as she shifted into defence mode. She made an attempt to laugh it off, the sound coming out jarring and false, but there was no choice but to proceed. 'But how can what they say be true? Sapphy has already left.'

He spun her out of his arms and left her standing there while his golden eyes glared at her in accusation. 'Who said anything about Zafira?' His question came as a harsh whisper, as a noose ever tightening around her neck.

Oh. God! She put a hand to her mouth as she realised what she'd done. 'I mean, I'm just guessing Sapphy was supposed to be the other party. It makes sense, doesn't it? If someone is trying to slander me, then naturally they'll choose someone I seem to be getting friendly with—a compatriot.' She was babbling, she knew, while Taj remained unmoved, his expression one of complete damnation.

She tried to brush past him. 'Maybe it's time we both focused on where the necklace might have gone.' But he caught her arm and hauled her back.

'When were you planning on running away? When you thought I trusted you so much it would be easy? When we got back to the city and you dialled up your friend to send a jet to collect you? *When?*'

'It wasn't like that,' she protested, trying to wrench her arm free.

'All the time you were sleeping in my bed, making love

with me, pretending you were happy, you were plotting to escape the first chance you got.'

'No! I changed my mind. I don't want to go.'

'How convenient,' he mocked. 'But that doesn't explain the absence of the necklace.'

She gasped. 'You can't be serious? Surely you don't believe…'

He thrust her arm away from him and she went with the force, happy to get as far away as she could from his anger.

'I don't know what I believe any more. I thought you were happy here.'

'I am happy. I have been.'

'Then why plot to leave?'

'Because in the beginning I *wasn't* happy!'

He glared at her.

'Well, what did you expect? That I would be thrilled I'd experienced the equivalent of being clubbed over the head and dragged off to some caveman's hole? You expected me to be *happy* to be told I couldn't leave, that you wouldn't let me? That I was virtually a prisoner here?'

'Then what's changed?' he demanded, his chest heaving, the tendons in his throat corded in fury. 'I have offered you neither a fare home nor a divorce. How, then, do you account for this sudden change of heart?'

She looked up at him, despair in her heart, her voice little more than a whispered entreaty. 'Can't you tell?'

'Can't I tell what?'

She made a sound of desperation—a sound that had to be rent from her. But still his face remained impassive, his chest rising and falling like a death knell. 'Don't you understand? For some stupid reason I actually imagined I'd fallen in love with you.'

'I told you, I don't need you to love me.'

She shrugged, holding her hands up in an impassioned plea. 'I can't help it,' she said. 'I love you.'

If only he hadn't snorted his disbelief. If only he had just listened to her, talked to her instead of storming away towards the bedroom, she might have stayed to try and convince him of the truth.

But he turned his back on her and kept right on walking.

This time her cry was like that of an animal in distress—a cry that echoed the feeling of her heart being torn in two—before she fled from the suite.

She didn't know where she was going. She didn't care. She just needed to get away—anywhere she could be alone, anywhere she could find sanctuary. He didn't trust her. He'd made that clear. He even believed that she'd taken her own necklace to bribe a passage out of here.

How could he? Hadn't he learned anything about her by now?

She found herself back in the orange grove, looking to avoid people while hoping the sweet citrus scent would find a way to calm the turmoil in her soul, and wishing, above all wishing, that she had never let Sapphy leave without her. After all, she had been found guilty of the crime. She might as well have committed it.

But Sapphy was long gone. How could she get away now?

How could she ever have imagined she'd be happy here? There was no point in staying if Taj had so little faith in her. And yet she'd believed at one stage that he loved her! She must have been mad to ever have imagined it. If he loved her, he'd trust her. But there was clearly no trust. Just as there was clearly no love…

She sank into a seat near a tinkling fountain as the afternoon lengthened, reluctant to move until she had some kind of plan, some direction.

And that was where he found her.

The crunch of gravel told her she was not alone. She looked around, her heart skipping even now at the thought that Taj had followed her. Maybe to apologise and tell her he was sorry.

But reality smashed that dream to pieces. It wasn't Taj. This man was of a smaller build, more wiry with a dark beard and calculating eyes. She stood up to leave the moment she recognised his mean face, but he called her name and she stilled, her pulse racing at being confronted right now by this man of all people.

'I have news,' he said.

She was grateful he didn't bother with pleasantries, because it meant she didn't have to return them. She had no doubt it was Qasim who had related the report of her discussions with Sapphy to Taj, having heard them from Abir. But why he had made up the lie about the necklace she couldn't fathom—unless it was designed to turn Taj against her, as Qasim himself seemed to hate her.

Even so, she stopped, her back stiffened as she turned to face him. 'I don't see why I should listen to anything you have to say.' She turned once again to leave.

'It's about the necklace.'

This time she spun around. 'Why did you tell Taj that I had stolen it?'

He bowed. 'My earnest apologies. It was not to be avoided. You see, I believed you would be so much more merciful than Tajik.'

His voice was so thick with false sweetness that she

wanted to throw up. She raised her chin, not trusting the man any further than she could throw him. 'What do you mean?'

'I know who stole the necklace.'

Her heart skipped a beat. If she could get the necklace back, perhaps there was a chance she could convince Taj of her innocence? Maybe this would prove that he could trust her? And wouldn't it be worth trying if it meant re-capturing the joy they'd shared until now?

She licked her lips, knowing that what she wanted and what she might get from this man could be completely different things. But one thing she did know was that she must not look too keen.

'So why did you lie to Taj?'

'I could not risk it.'

She shrugged. 'So you said before. Why not?'

Qasim shuffled under his robe like a man looking for excuses. 'Because, ashamed though I am to admit it, the thief is none other than my own daughter, Abir.'

There was no way of preventing her gasp of astonishment. It was the last thing she'd been expecting. 'But Abir is just a child! What possible reason could she have had for stealing it?'

The grooves either side of Qasim's mouth deepened, and he held out his hands in supplication. 'You must forgive her, Sheikha Murjanah. Even pity the child, if you will. She is young and weak. And you more than anyone must understand.' He shrugged and smiled crookedly. 'She took the necklace because it was meant to be hers.'

Dread crawled like spider legs down Morgan's spine,

turning her voice to nothing more than a coarse whisper. 'What do you mean?'

'It is quite simple,' he said. 'Before you arrived, Abir and Tajik were betrothed to be married.'

# CHAPTER TWELVE

'IT HAS to be a mistake,' Morgan said, shaking her head, battling to make sense of this latest revelation. 'Taj said nothing to me.'

'Oh, yes. This marriage feast was all arranged long ago. All that changed on a whim was the name of the bride.'

She didn't want to believe him. Couldn't bear to believe him. But even as she denied his words some horrible seed of doubt planted itself it her mind. There *had* been an awful lot of preparations done in double-quick time for a wedding arranged almost overnight—how had that been possible, if not for the fact that a wedding to another bride had already been planned?

But this was still Qasim she was talking to—someone who had lied to Taj about her. Why should she believe this man's word about anything? 'So why was it, then, that Taj married me and not Abir?'

Qasim laughed—an evil sound that thickened her blood to cold, wet cement. 'He simply changed his mind—as men in his powerful position, you must understand, believe themselves totally within their rights to do. The tribal chiefs were concerned for the ascendancy and demanding an heir.' Qasim shrugged and looked at her beseechingly. 'What could he do? He needed to marry someone.'

His words sliced her to the core. *He needed to marry someone.*

Someone.

*Anyone!*

She turned away, unable to look at him. Qasim was still going on about how she must not think too badly of his daughter. Morgan let his words sweep over her like a foaming wave, still too stunned to take note of any particular words.

So Taj had changed his mind about marrying Abir and then needed a handy substitute? Morgan had been that handy substitute. She'd been the one who was there, available, ready to be conned into taking a plane ride to a far-off kingdom and then to have the bombshell of this marriage dropped on her.

And all the time he'd made out that he'd chosen her, out of all the women in the world. All the time he'd pretended there was something special between them. What a joke. He hadn't chosen her. He'd damned near tripped over her.

But—worse than that—*he'd used her.*

Just as Evan had used her all those years ago, expecting her to marry him and lend him respectability. Charming, good-looking, easygoing Evan—who had never pushed her into sex, who had wanted to wait until the time was right, all the time knowing their time would never be right.

Evan had used her then.

Just as Taj had used her now!

She'd known from the start he wanted a marriage of convenience, but he'd never told her she was nothing more than his means out of an inconvenient betrothal.

*Nothing!*

Behind her Qasim bleated on, begging her for forgiveness, telling her he would return the necklace, while everything that had happened fell into place in her mind. No wonder Taj had told her Qasim had suffered a recent "disappointment". No wonder Qasim hated her so much. She could scarcely blame him. Morgan had probably broken his young daughter's heart even though she'd never wanted to marry Taj in the first place.

He'd made both of them suffer—made both of them unhappy.

Morgan dragged in a breath, the sharp scent of citrus no balm for her soul now. One thing was crystal-clear. Jebbai was just across the border. Help was as close as Sapphy. And this time Morgan wouldn't change her mind.

'Abir can keep the necklace,' Morgan pronounced, shutting Qasim up in an instant. 'It means nothing to me. But I need to get to Jebbai without Taj finding out. Can you help me, right now, to get there?'

His black eyes glistened before he bowed again. 'You are too kind. I will do everything I can.' He glanced around furtively. 'But we must move quickly.'

Barely two hours into the journey Morgan was regretting her easy compliance with Qasim's plan. Her leg was already protesting at the strain, and her head was thumping in the aftermath of an emotional day. But she hadn't specified a preferred mode of escape, and so when he'd presented her with a guide and a horse to lead her to Jebbai she'd hardly been able to turn round and say it wasn't what she'd had in mind—even when he'd told her it would "only" be a two-day trek.

But what did it really matter? she told herself. Right now escape and freedom were paramount. There was no way she could stay. She had to be strong. And she had more motivation than ever for seeing it through.

She'd gritted her teeth and hauled herself into the saddle, and, wearing a coarse robe to disguise her if anyone spied them from the palace, she'd set off behind her guide. It had already been approaching evening when they'd left, and she consoled herself with the thought that the temperature would be nowhere near as taxing as on the ride she'd taken with Taj, under the climbing morning sun.

An hour further on she wasn't so convinced. The mount she'd been given was proving to be no docile mare, like she'd had on her ride with Taj. And this was no casual ride. This was a spirited beast that seemed to want her to work hard all the way, controlling her on a ride that she had known would challenge her. Already her lower leg throbbed. Her thighs were not used to riding, making the strain on her ankle and foot extreme just keeping up with the pace, but there was no way she was going back. No way was she changing her mind.

This time, she thought, allowing herself a cynical smirk as her horse thundered on into the desert, following the guide, there was no knight in shining armour, or a sheikh in flowing robes, for that matter, to rescue her.

She had no choice but to keep going.

As she felt herself absorbed into the moonlit darkness of the night, trying desperately to keep sight of the white flap of her guide's robes some distance ahead, never had she felt herself so alone.

Two days in the saddle she had to bear. Two days to freedom. She bit back on tears of pain. It would be worth it!

What seemed like many hours later they stopped to camp in a tiny oasis with a few sparse trees, a patch of weedy-looking grass and a small dusty well. The ground was firmer here, near the mountains, with a thin layer of lichen and tiny grasses forming a crust over the sand. Morgan let herself down from the horse, staggering when her left leg refused to take her weight, and collapsing in a heap on the sandy ground. The guide barely glanced her way, making no effort to help, more interested in servicing the horses. Eventually he hauled two blankets from his horse, flinging one at her before wrapping the other around himself and settling down on the ground.

For the first time she realised how vulnerable she was. She was in the middle of the desert with a complete stranger—a man she had no idea if she could trust. A man Qasim had retained for her.

She shivered. 'No fire, I guess,' she said, struggling to ease herself into a more comfortable position.

His black eyes flashed over her.

'No fire,' he grunted in coarse English. 'Sleep now.'

'Thank you for doing this for me,' she said with a smile, hoping a few appreciative words might soften her guide's attitude. 'I'm really grateful to you.'

He grunted again. 'Sleep.'

She'd been sure she wouldn't—that she was too wound up with the enormity of all that had happened, that she would spend all night gazing up at the cover of stars that reached for ever and somewhere out there joined up with the night sky of her homeland—but a harsh shake of her shoulder and her heavy eyes told her she must eventually have fallen into some kind of fitful sleep at last. She remembered vague remnants of dreams—of Taj and Qasim and her sister Tegan. Strange dreams where hope and despair and loss were jumbled and interwoven, leaving her heart feeling heavy in her chest.

What would Taj be doing now? Would he care that she was gone? She doubted it. Beyond being furious that she had dared attempt to escape, his concern for her was limited to her breeding capacities. Too bad. He could damned well find himself another brood mare.

She blinked, trying to clear her head. Then she tried to sit up and instantly regretted it as her leg screamed out a painful protest. Other muscles unused to horse-riding were not helping. She squeezed her eyes shut. She could do this. She *had* to do this. It was only another day or so, and then she would be free.

Eventually she manoeuvred herself into a sitting position, already breathing hard with the effort. How was she ever going to get herself onto that horse?

A handful of dates and dried figs was thrust in her direction, and she pocketed them as she tried to ease the stiffness in her leg. It was hours since she'd eaten a decent meal, but right now she felt too sick from the effort of moving to eat.

Morgan looked around in the early pre-dawn light, surprised to see the dark shadows of a mountain range looming some distance before them. It was the same range she'd explored with Taj, she could tell by the ragged peaks. She'd never realised that the range lay between her and freedom. She just hoped they didn't have to go over it.

In no time it was time to mount. She dispensed with convention and mounted her horse from the right side, using her stronger leg to swing her weight up and over. Pain jolted through her at the effort of lifting her leg over and her left leg thudded down, but success was hers—she'd done it! She laughed out loud, tears tracking down her cheeks as she clamped down on the pain. Beside her, her guide looked on dispassionately.

'Come,' he said, spurring his horse into motion.

They walked on into the morning light, and as the sun rose higher in the sky the tolerable if uncomfortable ride became hellish, soon banishing all thoughts of laughter.

Her guide ploughed on towards the mountain range, seemingly oblivious to whether she followed or not, the distance between them lengthening as the mountains loomed ever larger. She felt powerless to catch up, the sun sapping energy from her with every step, heat and pain blurring her thoughts and vision, pins and needles assailing her weaker leg.

She tried to focus, searching the desert before her, hoping for a flash of white to confirm her direction. But the horizon blurred into a dull wash before her and she could see nothing—only the dark mountains growing before her, and beside them another darker cloud that reached high into the sky.

She blinked, trying to clear her vision, but the cloud seemed to be moving, bearing down on them, defying her focus.

And then, at the first sting of sand on her flesh, she realised.

*A sandstorm.*

Oh, God, where was her guide? Why hadn't he turned back to find her? Her horse snorted under her, flicking back its ears and tossing its head against the increasing bursts of sand. She tried to calm the beast with soft words, but her attempts were carried away on the howling wind, her reward a mouthful of grit.

She knew she had to find cover, and the fading shadow of the mountains was her only hope. Desperately she tried to wheel her mount and spur it into action, but the horse rebelled against her efforts to control it. Panicked, it reared up, throwing its mighty head around. She clung on as best she could, despite the pain that threatened to blank her out as the beast crashed back to earth. The horse was now her only hope. She had to hang on. But another burst of wind and sand saw it rear again into the storm, launching itself so high against the wave of sand that her numb foot could no longer hold the stirrup.

The horse stayed upright, suspended in mid-air for what seemed an eternity, as she called on every muscle she had to cling on, before it gave one furious bone-wrenching twist of its body and started a slow roll backwards.

She screamed as it went down, her foot coming clear of the remaining stirrup as she was flung to one side onto crusty ground that splintered like thin ice as she crashed into it. Frantically she did her best to roll herself away, before the horse thundered to the ground alongside her, its wild panicked whinny carried away by the howling wind like a trophy.

She lay winded, in pain and shock, managing no more than to pull her cloak over her head and stay close to the ground while she battled to recover her breathing. Beside her she could feel the horse struggling to right itself, and she lashed out with her hands desperately for the reins in case it ran away. But the horse fell back, time and again, eventually giving up and laying its big head down, its heavy chest heaving and sweat slicked from the effort, giving only the occasional nicker.

Fear clutched at her heart. If the horse had broken its leg neither of them was going anywhere right now. And where was her guide? Why had he left her to face this alone? And even if she survived the vicious sand, how would she ever get out of here on foot?

But at least now the horse was quieter. She edged closer, putting the horse's big body between her and the onslaught of wild screaming sand. She reached over to cover its muzzle with her shawl, to try to protect it too from the sand, and then tucked herself alongside it, reaching out a hand to stroke its mane and pat its side.

'We'll get through this together,' she told it as the wind howled and screamed around them, forcing the fabric into her mouth as she spoke. 'You'll see.' Underneath her hand she could feel the big animal's thudding heartbeat. It comforted her. She wasn't alone. They would make it.

Time passed. Endless time. She was hot. So hot. The air was burning, the wind endlessly howling, the smell of dust and sweaty horse was in her nostrils. Sand weighed down her cloak, where it formed pools in the fabric, sand clung in gritty tracks to the tears she'd cried.

If only Taj had cared.

If only he hadn't used her.

*If only she hadn't loved him so much...*

That was the truth, she knew. Those things wouldn't have mattered—nothing would have mattered—if only she hadn't loved him so damned much. That was what made it hurt. And that was why she'd had to flee. Because she'd truly believed he'd cared.

She'd *needed* to believe.

And now she was running away from herself.

That was why she was in trouble. It had nothing to do with Taj. What had he told her when he'd taken her to the mountain range that was now so close?

*"With me you need never fear. With me you will always be safe."*

He'd been wrong about one thing. Her heart had never

been safe. But she knew without doubt that if she'd been with Taj instead of her guide he would never have let this happen to her.

Taj would have kept her safe.

She had no one to blame but herself. Her crazy flight had landed her and this poor horse and possibly her guide in terrible danger.

Moisture she couldn't afford to lose welled fresh from her eyes, providing new tracks for grains of sand to cling to. But she had to be strong. She had to get them through this. She nestled further against the horse and let the slow, steady thread of its heartbeat reassure her. They'd make it through together.

## CHAPTER THIRTEEN

TAJIK hated sandstorms with a vengeance, and the feeling of powerlessness against the forces of nature for the second time in twelve months was making him feel sick to the stomach. He pulled his horse to a stop, cursing the wind and the accursed storm that had obliterated the tracks he'd been following. Before him rose the mountain range. Had they made it that far, or had the storm cut them down before they had reached there?

Neither option particularly appealed.

Behind him followed three riders and a pair of support vehicles. If they found her—*when they found her*—she might need emergency medical help and a speedy journey back to the palace. But he preferred to search on horseback, lest she was lying somewhere, thinly covered by the shifting sands.

The memory of the last time he'd been involved in such a search still too raw, too painful. Just one year ago a similar search of the desert had revealed nothing more than the scattered remains of twisted metal and fractured bodies. It couldn't happen to him again. Not so soon. Not now. Not when finally he had realised...

*Not when finally he had realised that he loved her.*

Finding her missing, searching the palace frantically and still finding her nowhere, at first he'd been angry that she'd run. Until he'd learned the truth. That it hadn't been escape that was planned for her.

And another truth had crashed home. She could not die—not now, not when he had finally realised how much she meant to him.

After the heartless way he'd thrust aside her declaration of love, he would never forgive himself if he didn't get the chance to tell her how wrong he'd been.

Covering his eyes with his hand, he scanned the desert, a movement catching his eye as in the sky some distance away wheeled a lonely buzzard.

A heart he'd never known could hurt so much slammed hard against his chest, squeezing bile high in his throat. He signalled to his men behind and set off at a gallop across the desert.

It was the flank he noticed first. The dark strip of horse-flesh just visible above the sand would mean nothing unless you were looking for a missing horse and its missing rider. They'd given Murjanah a horse that colour. Bunched alongside it poked patches of dark fabric, looking like nothing more than a bundle of rags amidst the dune.

He threw himself down from the horse, directing his companions to continue the search in the surrounding sand, and knelt alongside, his heart hammering, his whole body praying.

'Murjanah!' he cried. There was no answer. Gently he scooped sand from what appeared to be a cloak, desperate to uncover her, and yet at the same time never so afraid to do anything in his life.

He found a corner of the coarse fabric and eased it back,

only to be rewarded by her sigh, as fresh air met her flushed cheeks. Her eyelids flickered open in a confused squint. 'Taj?'

Something in his heart swelled that she should immediately assume he was her rescuer. Maybe he hadn't lost her yet? And then he scooped her into his arms, taking care in case she was injured. 'Murjanah, you are alive. I feared I'd never see you again.'

He spilled a little water from his canteen into her parched mouth and she blinked and tried to focus, her lips cracked and dry and painful to behold. 'You came for me?'

'I could not live with myself if anything happened to you.' He pressed his lips to her sand-crusted brow. 'Are you hurt?'

She gave a shake of her head. 'I don't think so. I just ache. Everywhere aches.'

He hugged her closer.

She tried to hug him back, but she was so weak, her strength gone. 'We made it,' she whispered. 'We really made it.' Her hand snaked out to find the beast that had unwittingly saved her life as she'd nestled into its lee. 'The horse?' she asked. 'How's the horse? His heartbeat kept me company, blocking out the sound of the storm. I think he may have broken his leg, but I told him we would get through this thing together.'

Taj looked at the sand covered carcass alongside her, unable to find the words to tell her. Instead he pressed his lips to her forehead again, letting them linger there until somehow she knew, bursting into tears in his arms.

He rocked her while she sobbed—rocked her for the loss of the horse, because he knew that she recognised what had happened to the horse could so easily have befallen her.

There was a sudden shout from one of his men at the

top of the dune. He turned to see a prostrate body slumped in front of the saddle of his man's horse. 'We found him barely alive,' he said in their own language. 'And we found this.'

He held up his hand, and a band of coloured stones sparkled and twinkled in the sun.

Morgan gasped, immediately tensing in his arms, and he could tell she'd seen the necklace too. Her eyes were suddenly afraid as she looked from the necklace to him. 'I didn't—' she said. 'I had no idea—'

He looked down at her. 'We will talk when you are stronger. Come,' he said, gathering her up in his arms, 'let's get you home.'

*Home.* The word held such appeal—but was it her home? She wished she knew. She was so confused, and so, so tired.

She dozed in the back of the vehicle, her head on Taj's lap. She dozed while gentle hands cleaned her of the desert nightmare and laid her in her bed, cloud-soft after her desert ordeal.

*Home.*

Taj had come for her to bring her home. Surely that meant something?

She opened her eyes, blinking into the light. Beyond the confines of the bed, Taj prowled the room like a caged lion.

'What day is it?' she asked.

He spun on his heel and looked around. 'Murjanah!' He rushed to her side, sitting on the bed alongside her. 'You've been asleep for almost two days. How do you feel?'

She tested her limbs within the confines of the bed. 'Stiff,' she said. 'Very sore.'

'Whatever madness made you flee on horseback, of all things?'

She pushed her head back into the pillow, taken aback at his sudden outburst when what she remembered of his reaction when he'd found her was only tenderness. 'I had no choice. It was horses or nothing.'

'And what if you'd damaged your leg? That horse you were on—it broke its leg.'

'Oh, God, the poor thing.' She shook her head. 'It reared up so high when the sand really hit. I think it panicked. I couldn't control it…' Her words trailed off as she stared unseeing at the coverlet. 'And then…and then then it just fell backwards. The sound it made—' She covered her face with her hands. She couldn't bear to think about it.

Taj stood and strode away, holding his hands out wide. 'Didn't you realise you weren't up to riding? And the cursed thing could have fallen on you.' He spun around to face her. 'It could have smashed your leg again at the very least. It could have killed you at the worst. Is that what you wanted? What were you thinking?'

She swallowed and gingerly pushed herself up to a sitting position. It was impossible to argue with him towering over her while she lay in a bed. 'I was thinking I had to get away. Qasim said he could get me to Jebbai.'

'You little fool! Jebbai is five days' travel in the opposite direction.'

It took a moment for his words to sink in. 'But… Why…?'

Taj looked coldly down upon her, his golden eyes polished like agate. 'Because you were being led deep into the mountains, whereupon your guide was planning to abandon you.'

'Oh, my God.' She squeezed her eyes shut as ice-cold chills racked her spine. No wonder her guide had resisted any and all attempts at friendliness or responsibility. He'd been planning to ditch her and leave her to her fate once they'd made it the mountains. He must have panicked when he'd seen the sandstorm coming, fleeing for his life and assuming the sandstorm would take care of his gruesome task for him.

Taj rushed to the bed, planting his hands down along-side her, his face just inches away.

'Were you really so keen on dying?'

'You don't understand,' she said, wishing her mind was clearer right now, not beset by the sweet memories of him rescuing her, muddying her earlier decision-making.

'What don't I understand?' he demanded. 'Why was it so necessary to risk your leg and your life?'

She shook her head. 'I wasn't planning on risking my life.'

'But you didn't mind sacrificing your leg? I saw how much it hurt you to ride, and yet you blithely launched yourself off into the desert, knowing you weren't up to it. Why? What possessed you?'

'I had to get away.'

'*Why* did you have to get away?'

'Because I don't belong here. I never did.'

'Of course you belong here. You are my wife!'

'But you don't actually want me. You just want a wife. *Any* wife!'

Silence hung between them like an accusation.

He blinked. 'Who says?'

This was ridiculous. She battled with the bedcovers, needing to get out of bed, unable to undertake an argument of such magnitude while she sat there and he strutted around as if she was the one in the wrong.

'Stay there!' he thundered. 'You're not strong enough to get out of bed yet.'

'And who made *you* the supreme ruler of the world when I wasn't looking?'

She staggered to her feet, feeling shakier than she was prepared to admit, given the circumstances.

'You see,' she said. 'I'm perfectly well.'

He snorted in response and paced the floor, raking the fingers of one hand through his hair. 'So when did you come up with this fantasy that I didn't want you?'

'When I realised that you didn't see me and decide you couldn't live without me. You merely saw me as a convenient alternative to marrying Abir.'

'That is untrue!'

'No, it's not! I was just a very convenient way of breaking off your betrothal to Abir. Qasim told me all about it.'

'I was *never* betrothed to Abir!'

Morgan reeled away. 'But Qasim said—'

'Qasim wanted me to marry Abir so that he would be closer to the throne. Yes, he had raised the issue with the tribal council, and they were anxious for me to start a family, and Abir's name had been mentioned. But I was *never* betrothed to Abir. Do you understand?'

'But the celebrations here—the palace preparations, the tent city—surely they couldn't have been arranged in just a few days? Surely there was another reason—?'

He arched one eyebrow high. 'Have you not dealt with Kamil? It would offend him to know you think him incapable of organising such a feat.'

Morgan let his words sink in. Because it did make sense in a way. Sapphy had been delighted Taj was marrying a fellow Australian, and she'd expressed no surprise during their time together that Morgan had somehow taken the place of another intended bride. Wouldn't Sapphy, of all people, have told her?

She shook her head. It wasn't enough.

'Even if you weren't betrothed to Abir, you admit the council were eager for you to start a family. Was it just a coincidence that I happened along then?'

He smiled across at her. 'It *was* a coincidence. The happiest coincidence of my life.'

'But you told me you'd chosen me out of all the women in the world!'

'And that is true. Because of all the women in the world you were the one sitting there next to my mother that day back at the Gold Coast, when I discovered my cousin's crazy plan. You were the one that made up my mind.'

She punched her arms into a robe as she started to protest.

'Don't you see?' he said, cutting her off. 'It's true. If it had been anyone else that day I might have embarked on a different course of action. I might have fought my cousin another way. But when I saw you I knew in an instant that marriage to you would be no chore.'

'But you married me on a whim,' she protested. 'You *used* me.'

'It is true,' he said plainly, and her heart sank. 'I selected you on a whim, and of that I am guilty. But as soon as I came to know you my thoughts softened. I wanted you to be happy being my wife. I wanted to do anything I could to make you happy.'

She looked up at him, afraid to believe him. 'Then why

did you turn away when I told you I hadn't stolen the necklace—when I told you I loved you?'

'Because I am just a man,' he said on a sigh. 'With a man's weaknesses. I was still blind to what you meant to me then. I was still seeing manipulation all around me. The necklace that was missing…'

She looked at him earnestly, needing him to believe her. 'I didn't take it. Qasim told me Abir had stolen it because the necklace should have been hers. I told Qasim that she could keep it. I never expected it to show up—'

He shushed her with his finger. 'I know. In fact it was Qasim who stole the necklace.'

Morgan was shocked. 'He blamed his daughter! What kind of father is he?'

'And he planted it on your guide in case you were both caught before your guide could discharge his grisly responsibilities. Then it would have proved Qasim's claim that you had stolen it to bribe your way out of Jamalbad, to further condemn you.'

Her eyes opened wide in surprise. 'How do you know all this? And how did you know where to find me? I thought you hated me when I left. I felt like you never wanted to see me again.'

He dragged in a breath and came closer, placing his hands on her arms. 'How do I know all this? Abir came to me. She had heard what her father was up to and feared for both her life and his. She had never wanted to marry me, despite his plans for her. When her father announced his latest plan to lure you into the desert, even love could not prevent her taking action against him.'

He paused and looked skyward. 'I was so wrong to mistrust you. I understood that Qasim was aggrieved that his plan to marry his daughter to me had failed. But I never believed he would put you in mortal danger. I am so sorry that I let his poison influence me. I am so sorry I put someone so precious to me at so much risk. I can *never* forgive myself for thinking so low of you—that you could have done such a thing. But when I discovered you were thinking of leaving, after I had thought you to be so happy, I could not believe that you would betray me like that.'

'But I *had* been planning on leaving,' she admitted. 'That much was true.' He opened his mouth to protest and it was her turn to shush him. 'That should hardly come as a surprise to you. You had brought me here under false pretences and insisted I marry you. What did you expect me to do? My arrangement was to leave with Sapphy and Khaled when they returned to Jebbai, even knowing what they were risking. But little by little you worked your way into my heart. And I knew I couldn't leave you. I let them go home without me, confident that you returned some of the affection I felt for you. But when you charged me with stealing the necklace I knew I had made a mistake…'

She turned back towards the bed, tears in her eyes as she remembered the betrayal and the bottomless despair that had driven her to seek escape—any escape.

'You weren't mistaken,' he said, his hands on hers. 'I don't think I realised it until you had gone, but you have come to mean so much to me, my little pearl.'

Slowly she turned her head towards his, hope flaring anew in her heart, while a seed of doubt still remained. 'I want to believe you, but even if what you say is true, will it be enough?'

'Why wouldn't it be enough?'

She looked up at the man she loved and the pain of

loving him right now was almost worse than lying half dead in the desert had been. To have him day after day but never to possess him—it would be torture. 'Because you're still in love with Joharah and I can't expect you not to be.'

He brought her hands together and squeezed them in his own. 'When you told me you loved me I couldn't cope. I hadn't been looking for love when I found you—I didn't want it if it would result in loss like I had known before. So I shut myself off from any chance. I buried my heart in my memories. You were right that I was looking for a convenient way to usurp my cousin's plans. And even though it's true that one look at you convinced me of my strategy to outdo him, I never expected you to take over my life so completely. You charmed me, you needled me, you entertained me in ways that I had never expected and I was enchanted. You uncovered my heart, a piece of which will always bear Johara's name. But until you left I had refused to acknowledge how much of my heart belonged to you.'

Happiness bubbled up inside her. She looked up at him, silently willing him to carry on, wishing he would finish what he was saying and tell her the one thing that she needed to hear above all others.

'So you're telling me?' she prompted at last.

He smiled down at her, the red flecks in his eyes glinting like fireflies. 'You are my sun, my moon, my starlit night sky and my shifting desert sands. You are part of me, my sweet Murjanah. You are my destiny.' He dipped his lips gently over hers. 'I love you.'

He pressed his mouth to hers and there was no way she could not return the kiss. Here was everything she'd ever wanted to hear and more. Here was everything she'd ever felt and wondered about. And now she was hearing it.

*He loved her.*

She smiled into his mouth, pulling back a little as he kissed her. How long had she waited to hear such words from him? 'I love you too,' she said. 'I love you so much.'

His golden eyes gleamed. He wrapped his long arms around her and pulled her in tight.

'I love you—forever.'

# EPILOGUE

THE desert palace was once again ringing with laughter. Except this time it wasn't a wedding celebration but a December family holiday that filled the rooms with joy.

Seated at lunch in an intimate dining room, Morgan swung her tiny niece up into the air. Ellie giggled in response to her flight through space, and the laughter was contagious. Morgan brought the laughing infant in to her shoulder, hugging her tight. It was so good to see her sister and her niece again!

Beside her Nobilah and Taj had been busy keeping Tegan and Maverick entertained, but now Taj took little Ellie and sent her soaring into the air again, She squealed with delight as she flew high, before he snared her once again in his safe hands. It was natural, Morgan knew, that while her family were happy she'd found a new home and new love, they needed to assure themselves it was a love they approved of. And so far, Morgan noted with no surprise, Taj seemed to be holding his own and more.

Twin small boys suddenly barrelled into the room before crash-tackling each other, desperate to show everyone which one was in charge. Their minder, Abir, came after them, her cheeks glowing and her smoky eyes bright as she chased them. They giggled as she charged, and dived away. Morgan smiled. Soon Abir would be attending college in Australia, not far from where Tegan and Maverick lived, a world away from her father's influence.

Taj passed the baby back to its mother and made a lunge, snatching up both boys in his arms in one fell swoop. The boys shrieked with delight. Their parents, Sapphy and Khaled, laughed as they looked on.

He was so wonderful, this desert king of hers. Looking at him now, she knew this man could not fail to make a good father.

*Which was just as well...*

She hugged her secret close to her. It was her special gift to Taj, and she was still so new to discovering it that she wasn't sure how to tell him. But seeing him here now, with the children, she knew that whenever she told him it would be the right time.

As if reading her vibes, he let the boys go and leant in her direction. 'One of these years,' he whispered in her ear, 'we will have lively children like these of our own.'

She smiled back at him. 'Maybe sooner than you think.'

He stared at her, his beautiful eyes glowing the warmest gold. 'You mean...?'

'I mean our baby will be born next August.'

The look on his face was worth it alone. The roar of triumph he made just a bonus. As everyone in the room looked on, he collected her in his arms and spun her around.

'Do you have any idea how much I love you?' he asked her when finally he set her back down.

'No,' she lied. 'Remind me.'

He smiled down at her. 'I love you like this...'

And then he kissed her.
And she knew.
He loved her as she loved him.
Forever.